*"Death makes angels of us all
And gives us wings
Where we had shoulders
Smooth as raven's claws"*

—Jim Morrison

A ngel parked the car and motioned for them to follow him up towards the sound of wild drums and rhythmic chanting in the distance. As they approached he and Hector fell behind Christie and Alexis, giving them a clear view of the night's feral festivities. At first Alexis thought they'd simply arrived at a Day of the Dead themed rave. Men in skull masks watched on as topless women painted like skeletons danced around a tall woman with a headdress made of colorful flowers and bones, whose face had been elaborately painted to look like a human skull. She wore a flowing white dress and was adorned from head to toe in gold, with trinkets and bracelets and rings glistening by the light of the roaring fire. In her skeletal hands she held a gleaming silver dagger with a long, bone handle.

It took Alexis a moment to see the bound, naked blonde girl on her knees in front of the garishly clad woman, crying and pleading to be let go. The skull-faced high priestess handed the blade to a man in a white shirt and jeans, who looked suspiciously out of place among the rest of them. The man wasted no time putting the deadly instrument to use. Raising the dagger over his head he plunged it down quickly several times, stabbing the wailing girl in her exposed chest. Alexis gasped as the gleaming blade pierced all the way through the helpless victim, sticking out her back momentarily in several places. An unearthly wail of suffering rose up into the sky like something dark and preternatural, the girl shrieking in abject horror and raising her hands to her face to ward off her attacker. It was no use. The high priestess laughed as her evil cohort brought the blood drenched blade down again, hacking the helpless girls left arm clean off at the elbow. The sound of her merciless delight sent icy cold shivers through Alexis, chilling her to the bone.

SAINT DEATH

by Devan Sagliani

Chapter One

A lexis could no longer feel her feet. The hot sun beat down on her as she listlessly shuffled forward, doing her best to simply stay conscious. The air felt like it was burning in her sore lungs as she sucked in a gulp at a time. A screech from somewhere above her caught her attention, reflexively causing her to jerk her eyes skyward. Overhead, two large, ugly vultures effortlessly circled her like something out of a Saturday morning cartoon. The image reminded her of sitting in front of the old, antique television set at her grandmother's house watching Bugs Bunny.

They're not really there, a voice in the back of her mind said, surprising her. *Just like the pixels on the television screen. Nothing is real anymore.*

She could no longer process what anything meant, not after what she'd seen. Flashbacks of the violence leaked through into her consciousness—a girl being stabbed again and again while she screamed, a young man writhing in agony as he was shot, a heavy fist hitting her over and over again—but she forced them out as quickly as they popped in. She'd shut down, gone into an animal state of flight for survival. There was still the wild panic climbing inside of her but no storm of thoughts to cloud her mind anymore, no distracting obsessive self-awareness to make her second guess her escape plan, just the strange, unfamiliar voice echoing in her empty mind.

You're only going to get this one chance, the voice emphatically told her. She knew beyond the shadow of a doubt it was right, but she was tired now, and every step was a battle. *Don't stop now or you will die a horrible death, and no one will ever know what happened to you.*

The muscles in her legs screamed with every step forward, having been pushed to the limit and beyond in the last twenty-four hours. She did her best to ignore the blinding pains in her body, pretending that she was a character in one of those "movie of the week" specials as she heroically trudged along. She told herself it was her will that moved her onward, but the truth was she didn't know how she was doing it—and she didn't care. There would be time later to think about such things, *if she made it.* In the meanwhile, everything had been reduced down to the essentials. All that mattered was that she somehow get back to the main highway and flag down a passing motorist. If she could do that she might stand a chance of surviving the hellish nightmare she'd fallen into. Then she could afford the luxury of contemplation. She was certain she would relive these harrowing moments again and again in her mind if she ever made it back home to Colorado.

No matter what happens now you will never be the same again, the voice cautioned. *Not after knowing what they did to Christie, what they'll do to you if they catch you again.*

They'd come down from Boulder on Spring Break, looking to get wild and blow off some steam, maybe even hook up with a cute guy from another school or better yet, an exotic local boy. Christie was more than just her roommate. In a lot of ways, she'd become the big sister Alexis had always fantasized about. She was what her mom used to call 'a bad influence' which made her even more alluring in Alexis's mind, having grown up a sheltered only child. While other girls were out drinking and losing their virginity at parties or back behind the Teen Center or in a car up at the Bluffs, she was cloistered like a nun in her fuchsia wrapped room, listening to streaming radio while surfing the web, dreaming of the day she'd be able to join the world she saw happening all around her on Instagram and Facebook.

It's the first thing you noticed about her, the voice cooed. She was bone tired. The only way to keep moving forward was to listen to the voice in her head, to let it distract her from the present by leading her through the events that had led her to this moment. She was only partially aware of the small clouds of dirt she was kicking up as she limped on over scorching earth leaving a trail behind her like a thin, crimson ribbon of fresh blood. *You hated her, and you wanted to be her at the same time.*

They'd both been fighting over a small apartment just off campus when it struck them they'd be better off splitting the rent and sharing the place. Alexis had always been more than just a little rough around the edges. A feisty redhead with short, spiky hair and pale white skin, her Irish temper got the better of her more often than not. She seemed to have a knack for saying just the wrong thing at just the right time. She was confrontational when teased, overly sensitive to criticism, and distrustful of other women in general. Christie, on the other hand, was a free-spirited party girl from San Diego with long dishwater-blonde hair flecked with flashes of gold, electric blue eyes that seemed to be drinking the color right out of the rest of the world and the kind of perfect smile you only saw on toothpaste commercials. She was the exact opposite of Alexis in so many ways! She had not just a killer body—somehow magically free of tan lines Alexis noticed the first week they lived together since Christie wasn't afraid to walk around the apartment naked—but the uninhibited personality to truly enjoy the benefits that came with it. Christie was the adventurous, curious party girl Alexis always wished she could be, if only she weren't so awkward and angry all the time, a trait she'd carried with her when she'd left high school but wished she'd been able to leave behind. After all, wasn't college the perfect time to reinvent yourself?

Two weeks into living together they were at a tense stand-off with no real clue how they'd gotten there or what to do about it. That's when Alexis had broken down and confessed how she'd been jealous of Christie's relaxed attitude towards not just men, or her studies, or her future, but life in general. She explained that nothing had ever come easy for her. She cried that she'd spent her childhood being ridiculed by girls as pretty as Christie for the unruly orange spikes sticking off the top of her head, her skin so pale it practically glowed in the dark, and above all else her lithe appearance bordering on uncomfortably bony.

"It's okay," Christie had said, shifting gears and softening. "You can talk to me. I'm not going to judge you. Go ahead and tell me how it all started."

The words came tumbling out of her so fast she almost felt like she was throwing them up. She'd always been skinny she explained. She just couldn't help it. She'd never been what anyone would call popular by any means but as puberty began to set in for all the other kids she went to school with she'd become more and more withdrawn.

"In high school the boys used to call me 'titless wonder' as a taunt about my less than impressive bust," she cried. "Long after the rest of the girls in my class were out buying fancy bras I was still looking in the mirror every morning at my puffy nipples for any sign of swelling. It was humiliating!"

She'd explained to Christie that Corina Rizzo, a snotty rich girl from Cherry Creek whose father worked in aeronautics, lead the other girls in making Alexis's life a living hell every chance she got. Corina seemed to effortlessly draw boys and men alike to her, with her exotic mocha skin and thick, lustrous black hair that always looked wet and shiny, like raven's claws. She was already naturally curvy but had gone up nearly two cup sizes over the long summer between freshman and sophomore years. She wasted no time rubbing it in when she saw Alexis, letting her know all about the extra attention she'd been getting from some of the cutest boys in school including Alexis's *not-so-secret* crush, Chad Richards.

"Men prefer a woman with curves," Corina gloated, cornering Alexis in the girl's locker room before gym with a circle of snickering girls like something out of a Stephen King novel. "Not a skinny little stick figure. From behind you look like a ten-year-old boy."

Alexis felt her hatred rising up in her like burning bile. It'd been a curse her whole life. She ate whatever she wanted but never gained any weight. Other women hated her for it, even though she had no control over her body. They called her a "skinny bitch" to her face, even some of the adults she encountered, unable or unwilling to disguise their disgust with her for naturally having good genes and a fast metabolism. At first, she would lock herself in the bathroom and cry but as time went by a deep-seated bitterness settled in, causing her to fight back. After all, what did it matter? They despised her no matter what she did, whether she was kind or vicious, so why not give them back some of the hatred and vitriol they so freely doled out against her?

"The only reasons you've got big breasts is because you eat too much junk food, you fat slut," Alexis fired back. "And boys are only interested in you because they know you put out by the way you're always throwing yourself at them like a bitch in heat."

She'd been expecting anger, but Corina's eyes seemed to light up with delight at her harsh words, as if she was happy to see that Alexis was finally fighting back, happy to have a reason to really dig into her with her skillfully sharpened claws and teeth and tear away a nice chunk of bloody flesh.

"There's a difference between flaunting what you got and sucking off boys under the bleachers," Corina said. "But I guess you wouldn't know that would you?"

"That never happened!" Alexis roared, her face glowing a fresh shade of crimson, the blood burning in her cheeks at the thinly veiled accusation that had dogged her since freshman year. Scott Kasbeck, a gorgeous senior, had lured her under the bleachers with the promise of being her boyfriend only to flash his penis at her the minute they were alone.

"Stop being such a prude," he'd barked in a hoarse whisper, wagging the semi-flaccid mushroom head at her.

She'd been unable to look away, mesmerized as much by the pudgy worm in his hand as the shock of densely coiled exotic fur climbing up from his crotch. She'd only just begun to develop soft red hairs down there. The sight of such raw masculinity left her dizzy and confused, which Scott mistook for some form of passive consent, putting his hand on the back of her head and trying to force her face towards his thrusting crotch. When she resisted he grew frustrated, pressing himself against her clamped lips and insisting she "just put the tip" in her mouth.

Humiliated she'd run out in tears, only to learn later that Scott had told everyone she'd gone way past oral sex and that the whole thing had been her idea from the start. There had been several other creeps that had tried to get in her panties as word of her being 'easy' spread across campus like wildfire in dry summer brush, which only fueled the rumors of her alleged promiscuity. The truth was she was still a virgin back then, but she wouldn't give them the satisfaction of admitting it. Knowing Corina, she'd find a way to turn that into an insult as well.

"Just keep telling yourself that and maybe one day it will actually be true. You know what you are? You're a carpenter's dream," Corina taunted, a malicious glint in her eyes. "Flat as a board and easy to nail. It's the only way you can get boys to notice you, isn't that right? By handing it out like it was free government cheese, which, judging by your clothes, is something I'm sure you've eaten plenty of in your lifetime."

The encounter had ended like all the others, she explained, with Corina and her circle of mean girls laughing and pointing at Alexis as she fled to the solace of the girl's showers for a long uninterrupted cry. She'd tried to talk to her parents about the persistent bullying she'd faced at school, but her father seemed squeamish to acknowledge the problem and her mother was far too much of a prude to understand. In the end she'd learned to suffer in silence, waiting for the chance to break free of her life and start over. There had been so many of these episodes she'd lost count. Each new humiliation had marked her, if only on a subconscious level. Each time she was attacked she grew colder, more distant, plotting her great revenge upon all those pretty girls for whom things seemingly came easy. Alexis had built a wall around her heart to keep the world out. She'd succeeded. She'd survived. The only problem was now that she had finally achieved the freedom she'd yearned for all those years she didn't have a clue how to begin breaking down her defenses.

"It's like I've become trapped being someone I despised," Alexis told Christie. "I don't want to end up cut off and bitter like my mother! I'd rather die first!"

By the time she'd finished relaying the painful stories of her childhood to Christie she was weeping in her arms. It was then that Christie had taken Alexis under her wing so to speak, making it her mission to teach her how to loosen up and enjoy her life more. Within a month Alexis was a totally different person, and not just because she had an expensive new wardrobe. They'd gone on so many double dates she'd lost count, swapped lovers, and even made out with each other once to win free drinks at a local bar. That was the same night Alexis got asked out by Chad Richards, who'd transferred to University of Boulder after flunking out of Penn State and losing his football scholarship. Alexis was surprised how quickly she got bored of him once she was able to wrap him around her pinkie finger. He was too clingy and too unstable to be real boyfriend material, but it felt good to know she could make him pine for her the way she used to pine for him. She owed it all to Christie and her 'leap and the net will appear' philosophy.

So, when her roommate suggested that they head down to Cabo San Lucas to soak up some sun and mess with the locals Alexis didn't hesitate. It was cold in Boulder and she was looking forward to feeling the warm air and gentle ocean breeze kiss her scantily clad skin. They'd spent all of three hours exploring what the resort had to offer before Christie had gotten stir crazy and dragged Alexis off to the local bars in search of what she laughingly referred to as 'fresh meat'. They'd partied their way through several packed bars including Cabo Wabo, Jungle Bar, Pink Kitty, Mandala, and ended up at the infamous El Squid Roe doing free tequila shots that were poured straight into their mouths. The roaming bartenders blew loud whistles as they funneled the burning liquid down patron's throats, then shook their heads for them. Alexis did two in a row the minute they got inside at the request of a cute guy in a USC shirt. Christie and she joined him and his friend at a booth but ended up ditching them early on after the frat brothers started arguing over which of them was a better athlete.

By the time the bar was closing they'd picked up two more suitable replacements. They were local boys who'd been generously buying them shots all night. Hector was the quiet one with sketchy eyes that never seemed to stop moving. He was short but strong with an enigmatic smile that only grew wider the more the girls questioned him. By contrast Angel was an outgoing social butterfly, even if he looked terrifying. He stood around six feet two and was covered in ropy muscles that bulged beneath his shirt every time he shifted in his seat. As if that wasn't intimidating enough on its own, his numerous jail house tattoos added to the sense of danger that hung around him like a cloud of invisible perfume. They started on his scalp, just visible underneath the short black hair that was growing out and ran down his arms like wet paint. The right side of his head bore blocky, stick figure letters that read Sureños 13. Underneath his right eye was a tattooed tear. On the back of his head were two glowing red eyes that followed you wherever you went and the words ALWAYS WATCHING.

He was dressed in an oversized black t-shirt, double or triple XL by the looks of it, that ran on past his waist half way down his dark-colored Dickies shorts. There was a blade tucked into the lower pocket, the glistening silver handle the only warning it was there, like a snake hiding in tall grass waiting to strike. His black socks were pulled up to his shins and below them he had on brand new black and white Nike sneakers. Behind his ear was a rolled cigarette. His sunglasses were flipped up on top of his head even though it was night and they were inside a club, which Alexis thought was strange at first. His arms were covered in a series of images from angels and saints to naked women with big breasts and low-rider cars and hundred-dollar bills. Most of these were crudely etched into the skin, the color of the ink a dirty ash brown like the kind inmates made from cigarettes mixed with pen ink and other equally toxic materials in the prison reality television shows she'd seen on cable. At each of his elbows were empty patches of unmarred skin, ringed by spider web tattoos that seemed to move as he flexed his elbows. Running down his wrist was a tattoo rosary that ended in another spidery tattooed web on the back of his hands. Inside more stick figure scribbles wriggled across his wrinkled skin like flies caught in a web waiting to be eaten alive. On his knuckles he'd tattooed the words PURO VIDA in empty outline letters.

Shortly after they'd invited themselves into the girl's booth, Christie sat in Hector's lap, claiming him. She had a thing for breaking in shy boys and deflowering geeks. Although Hector didn't seem like the typical kind of tech nerd that Christie liked to teach the ropes, his lack of reply was more than enough to keep her intrigued. That meant that Alexis was paired up with Angel, which was fine as far as she was concerned. There was something dark and mysterious about him that she yearned to explore. It was only after she began running around as Christie's fearless sidekick that she'd discovered this surprisingly reckless side of herself had been well concealed all along. She could no longer deny it and didn't care what other people thought. The truth was that dangerous men left her feeling sexually aroused and she craved that rush. Angel poured her a fresh drink. She stared in his dark eyes, her clit throbbing between her legs.

I wonder if he's rough in bed, she thought as the room began to swim from all the alcohol. *Will he leave marks on my arms? My ass? My throat?*

The thought sent thrills through her. They'd gotten into the habit of trying to one up each other, so when their new friend Angel had suggested they drive north to an all-night rave in the desert Alexis was the first to say yes. They took Highway 19 north towards Todos Santos. His car, a black Nissan Sentra gone dusty gray like a fading shadow, was so old she felt every bump in the road. Angel turned up the stereo, the blown speakers oozing electronic music into the interior of the jalopy like poisonous gas. After a while they turned off onto a bumpy dirt road in the middle of nowhere. Alexis remembered wondering to herself how he knew where to turn, since there were no markers. They drove in darkness, the sky above a brilliant display of milky stars twinkling down upon them with no light pollution to obscure them. In the distance she could see the ocean, the moonlight reflecting off the frothy churn of spume as the waves crashed and receded again and again. They turned right, veering towards what looked like a small village with metal shacks ringing a communal space and a large barn off in the distance. Alexis could just make out the silhouettes of a dozen or so men and women, like unstitched shadows running wild. They darted back and forth against the backdrop of the largest bonfire she'd ever seen, with flames that climbed like forked demon tongues towards the deep bruise of the foreign night sky, sensually licking at the stars endless shimmer.

You were more than a little drunk by then, the voice reminded her. *You'd been drugged.*

Angel parked the car and motioned for them to follow him up towards the sound of wild drums and rhythmic chanting in the distance. As they approached he and Hector fell behind Christie and Alexis, giving them a clear view of the night's feral festivities. At first Alexis thought they'd simply arrived at a Day of the Dead themed rave. Men in skull masks watched on as topless women painted like skeletons danced around a tall woman with a headdress made of colorful flowers and bones, whose face had been elaborately painted to look like a human skull. She wore a flowing white dress and was adorned from head to toe in gold, with trinkets and bracelets and rings glistening by the light of the roaring fire. In her skeletal hands she held a gleaming silver dagger with a long, bone handle.

It took Alexis a moment to see the bound, naked blonde girl on her knees in front of the garishly clad woman, crying and pleading to be let go. The skull-faced high priestess handed the blade to a man in a white shirt and jeans, who looked suspiciously out of place among the rest of them. The man wasted no time putting the deadly instrument to use. Raising the dagger over his head he plunged it down quickly several times, stabbing the wailing girl in her exposed chest. Alexis gasped as the gleaming blade pierced all the way through the helpless victim, sticking out her back momentarily in several places. An unearthly wail of suffering rose up into the sky like something dark and preternatural, the girl shrieking in abject horror and raising her hands to her face to ward off her attacker. It was no use. The high priestess laughed as her evil cohort brought the blood drenched blade down again, hacking the helpless girls left arm clean off at the elbow. The sound of her merciless delight sent icy cold shivers through Alexis, chilling her to the bone.

Without saying a word Alexis and Christie turned to run

back towards the car, but their dates were ready for them. Hector punched Christie hard in the face and she crumpled into a heap on the ground, knocked out cold. Alexis tried to dart past Angel, but he seized her by the wrist and began slowly dragging her towards the bonfire while she screeched like a bobcat with its foot caught in a steel trap, thrashing wildly about in her drugged stupor. Hector hefted Christie's unconscious body over his shoulder with a grunt then proudly marched out towards the high priestess, passing them as he went. Alexis scratched at Angel's arm, trying to free herself, but it only seemed to make him pull harder. She tried digging her feet into the ground and pulling back, but it was no use. She was simply not strong enough to fight him off.

A roar of approval rose up from the ghoulish crowd as the girls were brought in. The men greeted Hector and Angel like conquering heroes returned from war with human spoils for sacrificing. The killer with the blade placed it to the poor blonde girl's throat and sliced it open with one quick motion. Blood sprayed out in thick bursts as the high priestess held out a silver bowl to catch some, her gauzy white gown and golden baubles darkening with a scarlet-tinted shadow in the process. The girl's eyes rolled into the back of her head, leaving only the whites visible. She choked and sputtered momentarily before pitching forward to her executioner's feet and going limp. The high priestess of death showed no interest in her whatsoever, casually stepping over the dying girl to greet Angel and Hector and see what her good little boys had brought her. She took Alexis's face in her bony hands, examining her the way a farmer might look over newly acquired pig for slaughter.

"Get your fucking hands off of me" Alexis raved, but the old woman just smiled. She rattled off something quickly in Spanish, the words slurring together in a gloating thrum punctuated by rolled tongue sounds. Hector began moving towards the barn in the distance, Christie's limp body still draped over his shoulder, her wild hair blowing in the gentle ocean breeze.

Angel dragged Alexis by the arms once more but this time she wasn't going without a fight. She bit his hands and he screamed in surprise, before cocking back his fist and pummeling her in the face several times. It felt like being hit by a Mack truck. Alexis saw stars as blinding pain shot through her skull. She crumpled to the ground, but Angel wasn't done with her yet.

With a predator's swiftness he sprung on her, his face a twisted mask of rage and unmitigated hatred as he continued punching down into her face, his hard fists driving her skull into the soft dirt with the force of each impact. She was drifting away, slipping into a blackness ebbing up from deep inside of her, beyond where his fists could reach her. She felt cold, a numbness spreading through her limbs, her lips quivering uncontrollably before she passed out.

Chapter Two

Zack came to with a start, uncertain of where he was at first. He glanced out the window to see a rippling layer of ivory clouds rising to greet him like a quilted comforter made of soft white fluff. He wiped the excess drool from the corner of his mouth and blinked his eyes until the world came back into full focus. He was on a plane. It was coming back to him in pieces. He'd slept through most of the flight, the steady rumble of the airplane engines lulling him into fitful dreams.

I never sleep on planes, Zack thought, amused that he'd gone under so hard. *It's why I always choose a window seat, so I can stare out while we fly and keep myself distracted.*

He felt unusually refreshed for such a short nap. He stretched like a child, reaching out with both arms and yawning loudly with his mouth open. The plane hit a pocket of air that caused it to quiver momentarily like a puppy scratching a flea out of its ear and brought him back to reality with an unexpected queasiness. A moment later an attendant's smooth voice came seeping out of the overhead speakers.

"Ladies and gentlemen, we are now making our final descent into San José del Cabo International Airport. Please return your tray tables to their fully upright and locked positions. We also ask that you fasten your seatbelts for arrival and remain seated for the remainder of the flight. On behalf of the crew we'd like to thank you for joining us today and wish you a pleasant trip to your final destination."

Zack dug into his computer bag and pulled out his passport out, along with a form for customs and a tourist card. He vaguely remembered filling it out before passing out. He tucked the documents into the flap of his passport and slid them into his front pocket for safekeeping.

"Rise and shine buckaroo," an overly eager voice to his right said. Zack turned to see his childhood best friend Dave giving him a wide-eyed grin from across the aisle. "You ready to lose yourself in a haze of alcohol and hot chicks?"

Zack shook his head, his curly mop of unkempt dirty brown curls waving in front of his eyes. Dave held his hands up defensively as if to ward of the invisible cloud of gloom that had enveloped his friend.

"I know, I know," he said before Zack could protest further. "One thing at a time. First, we gotta get through customs and over to the resort. Then we'll worry about the rest. This is going to be the best vacation of our lives. We're going to burn Cabo down!"

Despite Dave's enthusiasm Zack wasn't so sure. The truth was that he wasn't really up to having a wild Spring Break party in Mexico but when Dave insisted that they go, promising to book them two first class tickets on his Gold Amex, he quickly found himself running out of reasons to object. Dave's parents had separated when he was a freshman in high school after it came out his dad had been having an affair with Dave's unbelievably hot babysitter. Dave's mother had a self-diagnosed nervous breakdown over what the neighbors were no doubt saying about her, and his dad had moved out and began dating a series of young girls not much older than him. He hadn't seen much of his old man during that time, but he didn't need to hear his dad's side of the story to know how he felt about it.

Shortly after that Dave started experimenting with drugs on a semi-regular basis and acting out in an obvious attempt to get attention from his increasingly distant father, who responded by throwing money at the problem and hoping it would fix things between them. It didn't. Dave dropped out of high school senior year, opened his own mobile car detailing business on a loan from his absentee father, and quickly ran up an insurmountable pile of debt which he tried to get rid of by adding cocaine delivery to his list of specials along with the wash and wax. It was all working like a charm too until one of his clients, a sleazy Persian mortgage broker with a thousand dollar a week habit, got pulled over with an eight ball while trolling for street prostitutes on Santa Monica Boulevard and ratted Dave out. Feds raided his office, seizing his fleet of company trucks and turning up enough blow to put Dave away for up to ten years.

Blaming himself for Dave's bad life choices, his father had pulled every favor with his well-connected friends he could, spending a small fortune in the process on some of the best lawyers in the state to get his sons sentence reduced. It worked. In the end Dave copped to misdemeanor possession and ended up spending six months in a posh rehab in the hills of Malibu overlooking the Pacific Ocean.

His father, attempting to mend their irreparably broken relationship, came to visit him every weekend. By the third month in it looked like Dave might be trying to turn over a new leaf—so to speak. He'd begun talking about wanting to go back to school and get his diploma but all that ended a few weeks before he was going to be released when his dad lost control of his Saab heading down the winding canyon on the way back from visiting Dave and plummeted to his death. Dave had become a millionaire overnight and Zack hadn't seen him sober a single day since. They'd grown apart while he was in rehab, owing to the heavy study schedule Zack had taken on freshman year at UCLA, but after his father's untimely passing Dave had grown paranoid of his new friends trying to rip him off all the time and had gone to great lengths to keep Zack in his life.

"Everyone wants to be rich, but no one ever tells you how shitty it is in real life having any kind of substantial wealth," Dave confided to Zack by his Bel Air pool over the winter holiday break.

They'd been lounging around all afternoon, drinking hard and reminiscing about the good old days when they'd lived on the same street in Culver City as kids. Zack's parents weren't well off by any means, at least not like Dave's were. His father worked in real estate and his mother in advertising for years before fibromyalgia had forced her into early retirement. But they were comfortable. They didn't flaunt what they had. They kept their heads down and worked and didn't complain. They'd bought into a quiet neighborhood when mortgage rates were low and seen the city explode around them. By the time Zack was getting ready to pick a college they had enough equity in their house and money in the savings account to finance his way through graduate school if he'd wanted to attend one. Zack assured them four years would be more than enough and to save the rest for his little sister Gwen.

Dave's parents started out just as old-fashioned as Zack's. His father, a software developer, believed it was best for a mother to be home with her kids instead of in the work force. He frequently dragged Dave off to St. Augustine for Sunday services saying there was "nothing more important than family" and that "the family that prays together stays together"—although his mother rarely joined them. Zack remembered how Dave used to have to come home early from batting practice on Wednesday nights during Little League season to have dinner with his parents for family night. Dave's dad was a typical middleclass family man in every sense of the word until he sold his pet software project to Microsoft for several million dollars and retired at the age of fifty-two. They moved to Bel Air, but Dave refused to switch schools, so Zack still saw him every day. Despite their newly acquired wealth and all the changes it brought with it Dave's family seemed to be doing all right for a while but about a year later Dave's mom walked in on his dad *in flagrante* with the teenage babysitter on the guest bed. After that everything went to hell in a handbasket quick.

"Yeah well maybe if you weren't living like a character out of a Brett Easton Ellis novel you might feel differently about that," Zack teased.

"What the hell is that supposed to mean?" Dave protested.

"I'm just saying," Zack said, palms out in mock defensiveness. "You throw wild parties up here twice a week filled with every kind of club trash imaginable like you're Mister-Less-Than-Zero. What kind of people did you think that would attract?"

"Well excuse me for not having weekly symposiums with Elon Musk on how to fix the world's homeless problem," Dave said, topping off his now empty martini glass. "In case you didn't notice, those parties are my way of meeting new women.

You were the one who said I needed to find a good girl and settle down."

Dave had been through a series of wannabe models and actresses over the course of the last year, each more terrible than the last. So far, the only thing he'd had in common with any of them was a mutual love of getting wasted. His last attempt at romance, Kendra, had been the worst by far. A failed model with aspirations of Hollywood superstardom she spent half of her time talking about what she was going to do once she "made it" and the other half name dropping.

"I'm pretty sure you know that wasn't what I meant," Zack laughed. "You'd have better luck finding your soulmate on a reality television date than you would with one of these chicks."

"Funny you should mention that," Dave said. "Kendra just got booked on a show where the contestants get naked and go on blind dates on some island. It's part of why we broke up. She didn't want the producers to find out she was seeing someone. She was afraid it would hurt her chances."

"You know what I mean," Zack said.

"I don't know who I can trust anymore," Dave sighed, looking suddenly older and more tired than Zack had ever seen him before. "Everyone is trying to get something from me except you. These days you're about the only one I feel safe around."

Zack had made it clear that he didn't want anything from Dave but his friendship, but Dave kept trying to lure him into adventures with his newfound wealth. They took a trip to Vegas a week later that turned out to be one of the best vacations Zack had ever had in his life. They ate in five-star restaurants, partied in the VIP section of some of the best nightclubs the dazzling city had to offer, and saw a UFC fight so close Zack was worried they'd get sprayed with the fighter's body fluids during the match. On their last night Dave surprised Zack by ordering several high-priced call girls to their suite and offering him first pick of the bunch. Dave tried patiently to explain for what seemed like the hundredth time that he had a serious girlfriend, Lily whom he'd met in his excruciatingly dull class on Milton, and that he wasn't going to cheat on her no matter how tempting an offer it was.

"Have you seen these girls?" Dave practically shouted, a devil's halo of white powder ringing both his nostrils. "They are some of the hottest chicks I've ever seen in my life. They cost five thousand dollars an hour. That's why they look like super models bro. If you don't get in there and pick at least one of them you're going to regret it the rest of your days my friend."

It had taken Zack nearly a half an hour after that to convince his old friend that while he appreciated the generous offer he wasn't going to ruin what he had with Lily.

"What's so special about this girl?" Dave demanded.

"I don't know man," Zack shrugged. "She's just different than other girls I've met. I think she might be the one. And if she is, and I cheat on her tonight, we'll always have this secret between us. It just wouldn't feel right."

Dave shifted gears after hearing that, slapping him on the back and telling him what a truly good person he was.

"You see? This is why I don't trust anyone else but you," Dave roared in a drugged-out stupor. "Every other guy I know would be in the master suite right now with at least two of those girls doing all kinds of depraved shit, even the married ones. No. Wait. I take that back. Especially the married ones! But you, you've got morals man. You've got heart. I can't tell you how much I fucking respect that."

Too bad Lily didn't think the same way, Zack thought, doing his best to fight back the bitter feeling rising in him again like a deadly viper. Despite his unyielding fidelity and devotion his beloved 'new center of the universe' had been sleeping around with several guys and using her friends to keep him from finding out by having them cover for her whenever Zack got suspicious. There was a distance that had grown between them as Lily became more brazen about her dalliances, and more callous and emotionally withdrawn from him. Right before Spring Break she'd decided to unload her guilty conscience on Zack. She told him that she had found Jesus, with the help of her newest lover no less, and that he had convinced her that it wasn't right to continue to lie to Zack. It was the last time he'd spoken to her since she'd headed back home to Missouri right after breaking up with him to see her parents and consult with her Methodist pastor about her budding new spiritual life.

Not knowing who else to turn to, he confided his utter heartbreak to Dave who, while being supportive and sympathetic, seemed elated to have an excuse to go out on the prowl with his best buddy. Within twenty-four hours Dave had rented them rooms at an all-inclusive resort in Cabo and booked the plane tickets. He'd been pointing out girls he thought might help Zack forget his girl troubles since the limo dropped them off at their terminal in LAX, insisting that the best way to forget Lily and move on was to hook up with the first hot chick he could find. Zack wasn't so sure. His head wasn't right, and he questioned his judgment along with his taste in women after what had happened. After all, he'd felt like something was off, but he'd let things go on anyway, hoping they'd sort themselves out in time. Now he knew he couldn't trust himself when it came to matters of the heart. He was surprised to realize, awful as she'd turned out to be, that Lily was the first woman he'd ever really loved.

"Don't look now but I think you've made an impression on someone," Dave snickered. Zack glanced back over his seat. There was a pretty blonde girl with dreamy emerald eyes and a tight Delta Nu pledge week shirt on staring in their direction from the front of coach. Zack quickly ducked back down in his plush chair.

"Well?" Dave prodded. "What do you think?"

"She's cute I guess," Zack shrugged.

"Cute? Are you out of your fucking mind? That chick is a smoking hottie on every level. Did you see the shirt she's wearing? She's a sorority girl. You know what that means don't you?"

"No Dave," Zack said feeling annoyed. "You're the high school drop-out. Why don't you tell me what it means?"

"It means that if you hadn't been so busy pouting and sleeping through the entire flight you might have already joined the mile-high club with her," Dave insisted, ignoring the petty jab. "She must have walked past you about five times since you passed out. It was like she wanted to be the first thing you saw when you woke up."

"So, what? That doesn't mean anything," Zack said, hoping to bring the conversation to an end.

"Um yes it does," Dave brayed. "You may not know this, being relatively poor and all, but ever since 9/11 passengers aren't supposed to leave their area of the plane. They say it's for security reasons but it's really just so rich folks like me don't have to share a toilet with poor commoners like you. Your girl keeps finding excuses to use the first-class bathroom. That's no accident bro. She's practically begging for it."

"I'll give you this. You've got a wild imagination," Zack said. "You think every chick wants it."

"That's because they do," Dave assured him. "They just don't want to look like sluts to their friends. That's why they wait until they are on vacation to show their true colors. Down in Mexico on some exotic beach no one has to know what a ho they really are. They can get as wild as they want and pretend it never happened. You wait and see my uptight friend. You're about to put a lot of new stamps on your pussy passport."

Zack cringed at his friend's crassness. Phrases like 'pussy passport' and 'dildo holster' had become common for Dave after his father's passing. Zack wondered if Dave even realized how off-putting they were, or how much he was becoming like his old man.

It's like all the qualities that he hated about his father are starting to slowly work their way into his new persona, Zack realized with a touch of sadness. *Almost like he's subconsciously turning into him now that he's gone. I just wish he'd be like he used to be back when we were kids playing in the streets until the lights came on, except on Wednesdays.*

"You said this vacation was just about blowing off steam," Zack argued, growing annoyed. "You said I didn't have to think about hooking up, that we were just going to get wasted and have some fun."

"I said that I would help you forget about Lily," Dave fired back. "I didn't say anything about not getting laid. In fact, the best thing that could happen would be for you to hook up with someone as fast as you can. That's the only way to get her out of your system man. Jesus fucking Christ. How many times do I have to tell you that before it sinks in?"

Zack grimaced. He knew Dave was just trying to help but once again he was taking things too far. It was Dave's way, and had been since his dad had moved out.

"Okay man I get it," Zack relented. "Just take it easy on me man."

"I don't think you do," Dave started but, to Zack's relief, the flight attendant cut him off before he could get any more wound up.

"Sir please fasten your seatbelt," the man said with a polite smile. "We're about to land."

Zack looked out the window as the plane began its final descent, passing through the marine layer of coastal fog and headed towards a long, semi-paved runway below. He closed his eyes, trying his best to ignore the sinking feeling in his chest, and waited patiently to feel the tug of the wheels as they connected with ground below.

Chapter Three

When she had come to Alexis found herself lying on a cold dirt floor inside a makeshift cell at the back of the old barn. There were iron bars caging her in. Her vision was blurred, and her head hurt when she moved. Above her, in the center of the barn, looped over a large wooden beam, was a single light bulb. It dimly glowed, casting pale yellow rays down over the darkened interior of the barn like a blurry smear. In the distance she could still hear drums and chanting. The grisly festivities were underway, and Alexis feared it wouldn't be long before the people who had locked her and Christie up came for them. Her face throbbed. Her lips felt painfully swollen and puffy, as did the skin around both of her eyes. She reached up to gingerly touch the tender flesh around her lips and mouth, gasping and pulling her hand back as much out of fear as from pain. She looked around to see there were several other cells, and Christie was face down in one of them. She tried calling to her.

"Christie! Christie! Are you okay?"

For a moment she wondered if her friend was dead, if perhaps they had already done whatever horrible things to her they'd been planning while Alexis was passed out, but then Christie let out a low moan and rolled over on her back. Her shirt was torn open and her breasts were exposed. She had a bright shiner ringing her eye, but not nearly the extent of damage Alexis was sure she now had on her face.

"Christie! Wake up!"

Christie tried to sit up but slumped over. She looked drugged and confused as she involuntarily made dirt angels, flapping her arms as she writhed on her back. An incomprehensible jumble of words issued from her pretty lips, like sticky vowel sounds drenched in gummy molasses.

"Dwheeryaamhiiiennjwhyyycanthife-fe-fe-filmuh-muh-leggzz?"

"I don't know what they gave us," Alexis croaked, her throaty feeling dry and raw. "But you're way more fucked up than I am and not making any sense. We're going to get out of here. I promise you. And we're going to make these fuckers pay for what they did. If it is the last thing I ever do we're going to make them pay."

"None of us are getting out of here alive," a strange man's voice said to the right of her. Alexis turned to see a shaggy haired hippie-type two cells over. He was around their age, but his sullen amber eyes suggested the cynical heart of a much older man.

"What makes you so sure?"

"Because I've been here for almost two days," the stranger said flatly. "And in that time the only people that have left have been carried out kicking and screaming by dark-skinned men with guns and knives. They don't return but you can hear them shrieking in the distance if you listen closely."

"St-st-stop it Francois," a girl's voice shakily said.

"Why, Karen?" Francois turned and leered at a girl in the cell nearest him. She was slightly younger than Alexis, with long brown hair and bright blue eyes. "It's the truth. I've come to accept it. You should too."

"What is this place?" Alexis asked. "Who are you people?"

"This place is hell," Francois said. "Or at least the mouth of it. I suspect we won't fully understand it before we're taken back outside and butchered like mindless animals."

"How is this possible?" Alexis cried in anger. "They can't just kidnap tourists and get away with it. Someone is going to come looking for us."

"Who?" Francois asked, an ironic smile creasing his grimy face. "Does anyone else besides your drugged friend there know where you are right now? Somehow I doubt it."

Alexis gulped as the sinking feeling returned to the pit of her stomach.

"We were at a bar," Alexis said. "They told us there was a rave party going all night."

"And you just left with them," Francois said matter-of-factly. "You never stopped to think about what might happen. You just assumed no one would ever dare harm an orange hair on your pretty little head because you're an American. Typical."

"Okay wise ass," Alexis said, feeling her blood rising in her face at his casual insults and at the same time oddly complimented by the fact he'd referred to her as pretty. "What's your excuse? Why are you and your friends here?"

"These aren't my friends," Francois laughed. "I know them as well as I know you. We're nothing more than victims of the same unfortunate circumstance, fools lured into the web by our less than gracious hosts. We'll all end up in a mass grave together or be dissolved in barrels full of chemicals like *pozolé*. That's all we have in common. That and the fact we all wandered off the path of safety at some point like fucking childish idiots."

"Stop avoiding the question," Alexis pressed on, her anger giving her new energy. It was quiet for a moment as she waited for a response. She could hear several people rustling around in their cages, silently listening to their conversation.

"Same as you," Francois said at last, his words like a pitiful confession. "I met a gorgeous local girl down at The Office, you know the bar on the beach? She told me her girlfriend had always wanted to have a three-way with a guy with a French accent. How could I resist? It's funny. When I told my family I was going to America to study they were sure I'd get shot. That's all you ever hear about America. Everyone has a gun. Who would have thought I'd die in Mexico on Spring Break instead?"

"Maybe someone else saw you leave with her," Alexis said, an edge of new hope creeping into her voice. "Did she drive you up here or did you take your own car?"

"Neither," Francois said. "She gave me some ecstasy, to 'enhance the experience' she said. At least I thought that's what it was, but a few minutes later I passed out instead. When I woke up my arms were bound, and I was being led to this barn by a tall man with bad tattoos and worse breath. I could hear a woman screaming but I couldn't see why. I know now. I wish I didn't."

"What is this place?" she asked.

"My guess is that they are a religious cult," Francois shrugged. "What else can it be? They kidnap college kids and sell them as sacrificial offerings to drug lords looking for some kind of supernatural protection, like black magic. It's not the first time this kind of thing has happened. There was a case with a premed student from Florida several years back as well in Mexico City. They took him right out in front of a bar in broad daylight. Mexican authorities later found his butchered corpse along with fourteen others, chopped up human corpses on a ranch not unlike this one, although in that case the cult leader was killed by police in a hail of bullets."

Images of the girl being murdered when they arrived flashed through Alexis's mind, but she forced them out as quickly as she could. Still her stomach churned as a wave of nausea overtook her.

"Devil worship?" Alexis shook her head in disbelief. "Is that what this is? Some kind of primitive Satanic cult?"

"Not in their eyes," Francois said. "Judging by the bride of death altar they've got out front and the way they're praying and making offerings to it I'd say it's Santa Muerte they are worshipping."

"Who?" asked Alexis.

"Saint Death," Francois said dourly. "Didn't you see the statue out front? It's the skeleton of a woman dressed up in a wedding gown, a sickle in one hand and a globe in the other. That's a dead giveaway, if you'll pardon the pun. In Mexican culture she is considered the master of death."

"How do you know all of this again?" Alexis eyed him suspiciously, wondering for the first time if Francois was really a victim like her or if he was somehow part of the kidnapping ring.

"I am an anthropology major," Francois explained. "Or at least I was. That's what makes this even more ironic, knowing that I'm going to die at the hands of one of the religious subcultures I've recently studied. There are millions of them in this country, but for the most part all they do is say prayers and make offerings. The poor love Saint Death because she listens but doesn't judge, but they aren't the only ones worshipping her. The drug cartels that have taken the practice and made it into something dark and terrible."

"This is insane," Alexis fiercely whispered. "I don't understand. What do drug cartels have to do with this?"

"The cartels have begun to demand that their foot soldiers make human sacrifices to Santa Muerte for protection and wealth," Francois explained. "They encourage them to torture their victims as part of the ritual and to take delight in their suffering."

"Why?" Alexis asked, her stomach churning at the thought.

"Control. Why else? They use their devotion to get them to kill their enemies without feeling guilty about it. The foot soldiers celebrate death by turning gruesome killings into religiously sanctioned offerings to the figure of death herself. Plus, it's a good way to weed out who the weak ones are in their organization. Anyone not willing to make a brutal human sacrifice can't be part of the gang. It's a good way to cut down on imposters and wannabe thugs."

Alexis felt a cold shiver involuntarily run up her spine. "What about the police?"

"What about them?" Francois replied.

"Sooner or later the cops are going to figure out that people are disappearing and being killed right under their noses," Alexis argued. "At the very least it's got to be bad for business, tourists being sacrificed by blood thirsty local cults."

"Assuming the cops are not in on it or being paid off to look the other way the chances are slim," Francois admitted. "There was a cult of Santa Muerte worshippers near Nogales that got busted a few years ago, but they were preying on ten-year-old Mexican boys. Even then it took years to break the case and the confession of one of the cult members. The terrible, awful truth is that we will join the legions of the missing, the unmourned, those who wander off from the rest of the civilized world and are never heard from again. If you are religious I'd suggest you start praying. Time to get right with God. Me, I'm an atheist, so all I can do is sit here and wait for them to come and take me."

"Sooner or later someone is going to come looking for us," Alexis argued, shaking her head as if she could keep his unpleasant words from crawling into her ears and sinking her spirits. She was unwilling to believe what he was telling her on any level.

"Sure," Francois said. "And then what? They'll hear that you were partying your brains out and went off in search of a drug-fueled rave in the middle of the night and vanished. If anything, they'll chalk up your disappearance to drug-related violence. Over a hundred thousand people have gone missing since the cartels began fighting one another for control of Mexico, including plenty of pretty American college students. Just look at the statistics. It's not all the media, making shit up to scare off tourism. This shit is actually happening. We're living proof of how fucking dangerous and out of control this country has become."

"Baja wasn't supposed to have cartel violence," Alexis protested. "The website for the resort said it was safe."

"And yet here we all are," Francois snorted.

Alexis opened her mouth to argue but a loud crash near the front of the barn caused her to jump instead, the words freezing in her throat, her skin crawling with goose pimples. Angel strutted in like a General come to examine his prisoners of war. He was followed by a short, dark man with thin black mustache and no shirt wearing tan Dickies shorts and a black belt with a large, matte-black handgun tucked into his waist. The man had tattoos covering every inch of his bare chest. There was a serious air to him that said in no uncertain terms that he was far more dangerous than his size suggested. He walked with the carefree ease of a hardened psycho, one who knows no fear, not even of death. Following close behind him were two imposing bodyguards both nearly twice his size in muscle.

Alexis scrambled to her feet, rushing to the bars and reaching through them to get his attention. "Please," she pleaded. "You've got to help us. We're Americans! There's been some kind of mistake! Please let us go!"

The short man calmly walked over and stood in front of her

cage, leering at her. The look on his face made Alexis's blood run cold. His piercing eyes were solid black, like two large bullet holes. Alexis quivered in fear, unable to shake the feeling of dread his skull-like features inspired. Her eyes left his and wandered down across pictures of dead bodies, names, weapons, and pictures of naked women all scribbled indelibly in his light brown skin. In the middle of it all was a large detailed Gothic cross with what appeared to be glowing light radiating from behind it. Alexis didn't understand how someone who glorified death and violence could also consider themselves to be religious.

"Juss whoodooyoo think you are?" Christie had managed to crawl part way towards standing by dragging herself up holding onto the metal bars of her makeshift cage. "When my fadduur findzzoout about this yoooar gunna wisshzuu whir nuverrbourn, youduuurtyfuukinn wetback!"

A smile of pure evil lit up the short man's face, causing the blood in Alexis's veins to freeze anew. He turned around and motioned to the cage with Christie in it. His bodyguards opened the door with a big skeleton key and began to drag her out. Christie tried to bat at them, her limp arms flailing about like overcooked noodles, her exposed breasts jogging back and forth. The larger of the men held her by a fistful of hair and punched her square in the face, causing Alexis to gasp as her friend went limp once more.

"No," Alexis cried, her voice barely above a panicked whisper. "Where are you taking her? Please no! Oh God please help us. Please!"

"What's the matter?" Francois roared suddenly, causing everyone to turn his direction in shock. "You fucking scared of taking on a real man you fucking cowards? You have to pick on helpless little girls because you got no balls? I'm talking to you, pretty little man. You try to act tough but underneath it all you're a fucking pussy. I bet you wouldn't last five seconds with me. Come on! Let's see what you got you fucking midget."

"Shut up Francois" Alexis screamed at him. "You're going to get yourself killed!"

The bodyguards shifted uncomfortably, watching their boss for some sign of how they should handle it. Alexis got the distinct horrifying impression that even the slightest nod would mean a nasty end for the nihilistic stranger she'd been imprisoned with. Instead the short man laughed, causing a fresh wave of chicken skin to crawl up Alexis's arms and legs. He walked over to Francois's cage, studying him with pleasure, like a spoiled child about to pull the wings off a fly. Francois glowered at him, not backing down an inch.

"Let's go asshole," Francois barked. "Me and you. Winner takes all."

The short man laughed again, a high-pitched sound that got under Alexis's skin like nails on a chalk board. He turned back to his bodyguards who joined in nervously like drooling sycophants fawning over a petty dictator. He took the handgun from his waistband, chambering a fresh round and pointing it at Francois' head. Alexis noticed Angel shifting nervously, as if his sneakers were suddenly hooked up to an electrical outlet. His eyes dashed quickly back and forth between the short man and his bodyguards.

"Any last words Gringo?" the short man snapped.

"Yeah. *Avale mes couilles grosse pute!*" Francois spit in the man's face, cupping his balls in a provocative gesture of insult.

"*Chupa mi verga tu pinche puto guey!*" The short man erupted in anger, dropping the gun down and shooting Francois several times in the groin. His eyes never left his victims face as the Frenchman howled in agony.

Alexis's screams were drowned out by the sound of gunfire in the confined area. It was so much louder than she'd imagined, not at all like it was on television. Her ears were ringing from the proximity. Francois slumped forward against the bars, sliding down them with a low groan of misery. The short man placed the barrel of the gun to his head and pulled it one last time, spraying Alexis with bright red blood and pieces of brain matter. She recoiled in horror, unable to process what she'd just seen, scrambling back to the edge of the barn's cool wooden boards.

Angel began to argue vehemently with the man in Spanish, gesticulating towards the bloody corpse now laid out flat in the cell not far from her. Alexis became aware that she was cold now, the little voice in the back of her mind letting her know that shock was setting in. She shook violently and uncontrollably all over. The terrible urge to scream again at the top of her lungs clawed its way up from the depths of her soul but she fought it back, knowing full well she'd only accelerate the inevitable. The two men argued like traders bartering over the price of a side of mutton. Eventually the short man produced a wad of American cash and thrust it at Angel, who thumbed through the stack quickly before pocketing the money and signaling they had a deal.

Alexis watched Christie for signs of life, but her friend was out for good this time. The bodyguards began to drag the helpless blonde coed away, her limp legs dragging in the dirt and leaving lines as they removed her from the wooden structure. The short man calmly followed them out. Alexis cried out to him in despair.

"Please don't hurt her," she wailed in agony, anxiety climbing through her chest like burning acid. "Please. Take me instead!"

Angel froze in his tracks at the sound of the words. Alexis fought the urge to piss herself as he slowly turned his head towards her, locking his glossy black eyes with hers once more.

"*No te asustes flaquita,*" he said with an evil grin.

"I can't understand you," Alexis cried.

"I said don't worry skinny one," Angel said, his English now barely comprehensible over his thick Mexican accent. "You're get your chance soon enough."

He blew her a kiss and Alexis recoiled in disgust. He turned and left. Alexis retreated to the darkened shadows in the back of her cell, her fear now a hard lump in her stomach. She listened for the sound of her friends tortured screams but never heard them. For a while she imagined that Christie might have escaped and gone for help. She closed her eyes and did her best to ignore the smell that had begun to waft down from the cell with Francois' decomposing corpse. Hours went by, but Christie never returned. She wept until she no longer had tears, until every ounce of self-pity had left her, and the dry sobs gave way to a feeling of perpetual dread.

He's right, the voice told her as she trembled uncontrollably. *Your time is almost up.*

Chapter Four

The line through customs was longer than Zack expected, but despite Dave's constant bitching they managed to work their way to the front in a decent amount of time. That's when the trouble started. The customs official barely gave Zack's passport a second glance and didn't ask him any questions at all, but when Dave got to the counter the whole line stopped for nearly ten full minutes as they examined all his paperwork in detail. Two guards came over and went through all his stuff, pulling it out and checking his carry on for any secret compartments. Zack felt like his guts were full of heavy cement as he watched in fear as they fired one question after another at his travel companion.

"Where are you coming from Señor?" asked the official in a monotone voice.

"Los Angeles," responded Dave.

"Where are you staying?" the official prodded.

"Cabo San Lucas," Dave laconically replied, offering nothing more.

"Which resort?" the official probed further.

"It's on my paperwork," Dave said, doing his best to fight back his building anger.

"And do they know you are staying there?" the official demanded, pouring back over Dave's paperwork again.

"I sure hope so," Dave said sarcastically, his voice rising several octaves in frustration. "Considering I've already paid for the full week. That's generally how things work in my limited experience."

"So, if I were to call them they would verify that you are a confirmed guest?" the official asked accusingly.

"How many ways are there to say this? Yes. Do I have to spell it out for you?" Dave looked like he was doing everything in his power to keep from losing his calm and screaming in the man's face. Zack wondered how long his friend could hold up under this kind of treatment before he finally snapped. He knew it would get ugly for both of them if that happened.

"And you are not just giving us a fake address, so you can go about other business while you are here?" the official asked, staring hard at Dave.

"I'm not here on business," Dave said, his face turning beet red as his temper began to flare. "I'm here on vacation. You know? Spring Break? Pretty girls and buckets of cervezas? *Comprende amigo?*"

Zack looked back at the line of impatient college students waiting to make their way through security to see the girl in the Delta Nu sweatshirt staring at him. She was the only one still smiling, although it looked more like sympathy than excitement. They made eye contact briefly before he turned away, a feeling of guilt and self-loathing crashing over him for liking her.

Jesus man, he thought. *It's not like I'm still with Lily so why do I feel so guilty? Hell, after what she's done I have every right to look at other women. Dave's right about that, even if the way he put it was way grosser than I would. I may not be ready to hook up with someone new but at least I can enjoy a little extra attention without feeling like a total dirt bag.*

It was no use. The truth was that his heart still hurt. He knew that meant that he still loved Lily, that he belonged to her in some way, even if she no longer wanted what he had to offer. He thought about what she'd said to him, the words burning a hole right through him. It was all so unreal. How could she treat him like that? He was one of the good guys, wasn't he? He resolved that he'd try, and that just because he wasn't ready to stamp out his 'pussy passport' didn't mean he couldn't have fun flirting with cute girls, especially if they started it. Besides this vacation was a dream come true for him, something he'd never have been able to afford on his own. There was no point in spending it moping over a girl who couldn't even be trusted when she did want to be with him. He resolved that he'd try harder to put Lily behind him and go on with his life.

Who knows? Maybe this vacation is exactly what I need after all.

Zack turned back to Dave, who by this point was working himself into a full lather.

"Calm down sir," the official said, signaling for more officers.

"I will not calm down," Dave shouted. "This is outrageous. I've got rights! You're treating me like I fucking brought a bomb in my carry on, like I'm a terrorist or something! It's fucking bullshit!"

"Turn around and put your hands behind your back now," a commanding voice said. Dave spun around to see several officers were making a beeline directly for him, the biggest of which was closing in cuffs already in hand. They formed a small semi-circle in the off chance he decided to make a run for the door. Dave shook his head in disbelief but complied with their orders. "This is unbelievable. You guys are something else."

The customs official ignored him, picking up the phone in his booth and listening as someone gave him further instructions. Zack got the distinct impression that they were intentionally messing with Dave, giving him a hard time and causing him extra delays for their own amusement. He was just beginning to wonder if they would make it into Mexico at all when the customs official finally relented and stamped Dave's passport. He motioned for the officer to uncuff him, but before he could Dave stepped forward, bringing his arms around front of him with the open cuffs dangling from one wrist. "Ta da!"

The burly officer wasn't amused. He snapped Dave's hand down hard before unlocking the second cuff and pocketing them. He glared at Dave who stepped past him and held out his hand for his passport, but the customs official took his time passing it back to him.

"Be careful while you are here, Señor," the man said ominously. "And remember that we take narcotics charges very seriously in Mexico. You will not get another warning."

Dave snatched his passport out of the man's hand, shooting him a cross look before walking over to his violated luggage. He mumbled a series of unforgivable curses under his breath as he quickly stuffed his belongings back into his bags and headed for the exit. Zack had to hustle to keep up with him. Once they were outside Dave made his way down towards the end of the taxi line. Zack dogged him as they passed a line of college kids with earbuds or Beats on, all listening to music as they waited.

"What was that all about?" Zack asked.

"It's bullshit man," Dave shouted. "I got busted one time in Tijuana with a joint. The cop made us sit in the cell for an hour then asked for a bribe. It wasn't even supposed to go on my record but obviously that was a fucking lie too. They've red flagged me. There is no way that was random."

"Since when do you smoke weed?"

"I don't," Dave erupted. "You know that. That's the most fucked up part about this whole story. Kendra kept saying she wanted some and I kept telling her it was a waste because all she was likely to find was Mexican dirt weed when she was used to smoking Humboldt green. Instead I got hauled off to jail and you wanna know the worst part? She left me there and took a cab back to our hotel in San Diego! Can you believe that?"

"That's crazy," Zack said lamely, not sure how to comfort his friend. "Well it's over now. Let's grab a cab and get over to the resort. I'm itching to try the swim up bar. First drinks on me."

"It's all inclusive man," Dave reminded him. "Which means all the drinks are technically on me."

"Either way," Zack said, pushing his bags into the cab line, "you definitely need a drink."

"What are you doing?" Dave asked, still hot from his run in with the customs official.

"I'm getting in line before all the angry people behind us make their way out here," Zack patiently explained.

"Fuck that. I'm not taking a cab all the way there," Dave said.

"What's all the way there?" Zack asked. "We're in Cabo. How far is the resort?"

"Dude," Dave guffawed, the first hint of a smile returning to his face. "The airport is like almost an hour from town. I'm not sitting in some stinky cab with broken AC all the way there. No way. It's hot as shit out here. Let's go find ourselves a better form of transportation."

Dave turned and made his way down further to where a stretch of concrete separated the main road from the pick-up area. Once again Zack scurried after him. There was a black limo parked some ways down. The driver, dressed in a pressed white shirt, dark slacks and shades, was arguing with a tall blond kid in a bright neon tank top and retro 80's sunglasses. The sun glistened off the chauffeur's shaved head as beads of sweat rolled down his neck, running over what looked like an old gang tattoo barely covered by his wilting shirt color. Zack could just make out what they were saying as he approached.

"I told you," the driver informed the irate blond man wearing a loud Hawaiian shirt. "It's a hundred American dollars cash. That includes AC and a full wet bar. That's a very good price."

"Come on buddy," the guy haggled, his voice taking on a note of condescension. "I'll give you sixty bucks. Take it or leave it. That's a pretty good deal for you and you know it. It's probably more than your whole family makes in a month. Besides, it's not like you've got people lining up to beg you for a ride."

"I'll give you a hundred dollars cash just to get out of this heat," Dave said with a shit eating grin. He held up the money and waved it for effect.

The driver turned to the guy he'd been arguing with whose face was now contorted with fresh anger. "You were saying?"

"Fuck off man," the man angrily spat at Dave. "I was here first. Mind your own business asshole."

"We're ready to go now," Dave plowed on ignoring him. "That is if you're available."

"You can't just come along and snake my ride man," the guy pouted, puffing his chest up in a comical display of masculinity. "We were in the middle of negotiating here."

Zack noticed that while the angry stranger had intimidating biceps his gym workout clearly overlooked his lower half. His scrawny little chicken legs looked easy enough to kick out from underneath him in the event a real fight broke out. Zack had saved Dave from more than one fight he'd picked over the years, so he was used to going into defense mode. The driver ignored the bully's whining and took the crisp bill from Dave's hands.

"Let's go," he said. Dave and Zack walked around to the back of the limo. The driver opened the trunk and helped them put their luggage in. The blond guy, not used to not getting his way, followed them the whole-time whining.

"Now wait a minute," he said, looking desperate. "I'll pay the hundred. I'm sorry. Just give me a minute. My friends should be out through customs any minute now. I don't know what the holdup is."

"*Lo siento*," the driver said, opening the door so that Zack and Dave could climb inside. "Time is money for us poor people. I'm sure you understand. Better luck next time *Güero*."

"You can't do this!" the blond guy indignantly roared.

"I believe I already have," he replied, walking past him and slipping behind the wheel of his limo. The driver turned on the car and all at once deliciously cool air conditioning replaced the hot sticky feeling that had enveloped them since they'd stepped outside of the airport. The angry loser slammed his fist onto the hood of the limo before storming off in a huff. The driver watched him go for a few seconds, then turned to his new passengers.

"Wow," Zack said. "What an asshole. I hope you don't think all Americans are like that."

"Actually, I was born and raised in Chicago," the driver said with a smile, his English now dramatically improved. "My mom is American, but my father was from here in Baja. I spent most of my life in America before coming here a few years back. The truth is I was enjoying seeing him get worked up. Names Oscar. Where to?"

"We're headed to Cabo," Zack said.

"That much I assumed," Oscar chuckled, pulling out into traffic and turning on the radio. Rap music mixed with electronica filled the car, but Zack wasn't familiar with any of it. All the words were in Spanish.

"Sorry," Oscar said, seeing Zack's reaction and turning the radio down. "I'm addicted to Reggaetón. Any place in particular?"

"Anywhere near resort row is fine," Dave clarified.

"Not a problem," Oscar said. "I've got cold water back there, *cerveza*, and some Patron. If you need anything stronger let me know."

"Well now that you mention it," Dave began, but Zack cut him off before he could get a pharmaceutical request out.

"Dave," Zack said sternly, giving his friend a dirty look.

"What?" Dave asked, feigning innocence.

"You know what," Zack fired back at him, not backing down an inch. "You barely made it through security. Are you sure you want to start screwing around already?"

"So, I like cocaine," Dave said. "Does that make me a bad guy? Besides, as you and the rest of the flight we were just on now know I don't have anything on me. If I'd have had so much as a generic aspirin in my luggage they would have found it and hauled me off to the pokey."

"Can you wait just a day? That's all I'm asking. I'd just like to get settled in before you start risking our entire trip for your drug habit," Zack pleaded.

"Fine," Dave relented, "but if I end up not being able to score later I'm going to kick your ass."

"You can try," Zack said with a smile. He and Dave had gotten into it more than once over the years, both playfully and twice out of real anger. And every time Zack had easily overpowered his smaller friend. Dave's real strength didn't come from knowing how to handle himself in a fight so much as knowing how to talk his way out of one, hence his need for Zack to bail him out of all the trouble his big mouth had gotten them both into over the years.

"Here," Oscar said, handing them each a business card. "If you need anything just call me and I will bring it to you."

Zack tried to hand his back, but Oscar wouldn't take it.

"I don't need one," Zack insisted. "I don't party."

"Keep it," Oscar said with a wink. "In case your friend loses his. Sooner or later everything gets lost or stolen here, even from the resorts. Best to keep your passports and other valuables on you at all times. And whatever happens do not score on the street or the beach. There are undercovers everywhere looking to take advantage of dumb Americans. They'll sell you an eight ball and then have their partner pick you up and extort every last dime you've got on you. I've seen it countless times."

"Trust me I know," Dave groaned.

"I still can't believe that the cops do that," Zack said.

"They don't make much," Oscar explained. "So, they have to make it up somewhere and not just with tourists. I get pulled over twice a week and I'm from here. One way or another they get their cut."

"How is that legal?" Zack asked, perplexed.

"It's just how things work here," Oscar shrugged. "It's called *La Mordida,* or the bite. It's become so engrained in our system no one even bothers to complain, except *turistas.* The Commandante turns a blind eye so long as he gets his cut of the action. Down here he is the law of the land. The only person he answers to is the Governor. Everyone else follows his lead in a 'shit flows downhill' kind of way."

"What happens if you don't have more than a few bucks on you?" Zack was hoping he wouldn't have to find out during their stay, but he also knew how relentless Dave was. He figured it was better to understand how things worked just in case his friend landed them both in hot water again.

"I've heard some of them will take you back to your hotel to search for more," Oscar said. "Others might just take you out to a deserted stretch of road, kick the shit out of you, and leave you to find your way back home. Then again, there is always the possibility they will leave you to rot in a Mexican jail."

"That's all bullshit," Dave chuckled. "Mexican prisons aren't all that different from American ones. I got hauled in once in tee-jay."

"You got taken in to the station," Oscar corrected. "Prison is much, much worse."

"So that's not just an old wives tale?" Dave asked.

"I assure you it isn't," Oscar said, a knowing look in his eyes. "I spent five years in a super max up in Chicago. One of the toughest places I ever did time. It was a piece of cake compared to the two weeks I did in Sinaloa. At least they feed you in America. Three hots and a cot, even with overcrowding.

Not to mention cable TV. Down here you get crammed in a cell with a bucket. If you're friends and family don't bring you food, you starve. And don't even think about catching a cold, because by the time they get a doctor to give you a check-up you'll most likely be dead from whatever made you sick in the first place."

"What did you do time for in Chicago, if you don't mind me asking?" Dave shot Zack a look as if to say he'd gone too far.

"It's cool," Oscar casually replied, seeing the tense exchange between them. "I don't mind talking about it. Assault with a deadly weapon, plus several probation violations they tacked on, and possession."

"Wow," Zack said, hoping in the back of his mind that Oscar had truly changed his ways and wasn't planning on robbing and killing them before dumping their bodies in a ditch on the side of the road.

"That's crazy man," Dave added.

"I'm lucky," Oscar said. "Got into a bar fight one night and shit got out of hand. I put five shots into a rival gang member, but the guy lived somehow, which is a fucking miracle. If he hadn't I would still be locked up. Prison changed my life."

"How so?" Dave asked.

"Before that all I cared about was partying all the time, getting in trouble," Oscar told them. "I had no plan for the future. I ran with the wrong people and made one bad choice after another. Shit gets crazy when you're out on the streets every day. Always something going down. Always some new trouble. You're surrounded by your boys and you don't have time to think about the consequences of your actions. In prison I got plenty of time to do just that—to think. I decided I didn't want to live like that anymore. I was losing too many friends. Life didn't have any meaning. I was just waiting to die. I decided that when I got out I would come back home and start my own business."

"Good for you man," Dave said in a congratulatory tone.

"It's been all right," Oscar shrugged. "Always plenty of rich people looking for a fancy ride into town."

"I hope they're not all like that guy that was arguing with you when we first saw you," Zack said.

"Mostly they're like you but every now and then I get lucky and it's a bunch of cute girls all giggling and changing into bikinis," Oscar bragged.

"Nice," Dave said.

"I'm going to roll up the window, so you can just kick back and relax," Oscar said. "We'll be there in no time."

Oscar closed the partition between them while Dave fiddled with the radio dial in the back. Zack held his breath, waiting to be inundated with some other kind of rap music, but was pleasantly surprised when good old American rock and roll came out of the speakers instead in the form of Mick Jagger wailing about giving the devil a break. Dave poured them both a shot of chilled tequila from the mini bar. He held one out for Zack, who reluctantly took it. Dave clinked the glasses a little harder than he intended to as a pothole caused the car to unexpectedly jump. They both laughed, pleasantly surprised that their drinks hadn't been lost in the commotion.

"Here's to a Spring Break none of us will ever forget!" Dave said, wasting no time slamming down his shot immediately after the toast. He stared at Zack who was still holding his glass. "Well? You gonna hold onto that thing all day or are you planning on drinking it?"

Zack nodded then slammed the shot as fast as he could, tilting his head back to get it all down at once. It burned in his throat, but he fought off the involuntary tears welling up in his eyes. Dave laughed and poured them both another shot.

"Take it easy man," Zack said. "We just got here."

"Just trying to get my money's worth," Dave protested, raising his shot over his head. "To Cabo!"

"To Cabo," Zack answered back, clinking glasses once more and slamming back his shot. "And all the hot chicks in bikinis you can shake your dick at."

"Amen to that brother," Dave laughed. "A-fucking-men!"

Chapter Five

The heat was already starting to make her dizzy as she stumbled along, listening to the little voice in her head.

You'd still be in that awful cell, the voice reminded her again, *had I not come up with a plan to escape. If I had just given up the way you keep trying to you'd be waiting to be dragged off like your friend was and murdered.*

Her mind flashed back again to that awful place. Alexis had managed to work one of the boards in the back of her cell loose, the salty ocean air from the nearby pounding surf having caused the bottom of the wood to rot out in crumbling pieces. She'd dug into the damp, cool soil with her fingers, ignoring the blinding pain in her hands as she tunneled into the ground like an animal. Every few hours another "customer" would arrive and select a fresh victim. Alexis was grateful for once to be overlooked, even if a wave of guilt and shame crashed over her each time they dragged another one off kicking and screaming. She'd worked all night, goaded on by the sound of blood curdling screams outside as much as the pitiful whimpering of the others locked in the adjoining cell, the blubbering and pleading somehow amplified by the complete darkness of her surroundings.

"Please," the voices cried out. "Please just let me go home! I just want to go home!"

Don't stop digging, the voice had told her then. *This is your one shot!*

She thought of Corina for some reason as she pushed herself to dig faster. She'd just managed to make enough space to wriggle painfully under and escape by the time the first rays of light were beginning to fill the sky. Getting to her feet she heard a wail of agony coming from where she'd arrived as the girl next to Francois—Karen he'd called her—was butchered alive in front of the grim skeletal statue. Her killer took a steaming pile of entrails from the fresh gash he'd made in her stomach and held the slick guts over his head in triumph while the crowd roared in appreciation.

Don't pass out, the voice warned her. *Block it out or you're a goner.*

The morning air smelled acrid, like burned meat mingled with marijuana smoke. Alexis knew she had no time left to waste with fear or panic. It was just a matter of minutes before they came looking for her, the only one left to sell for slaughter.

Who would have thought you'd ever be glad to be picked last? She chuckled to herself, feeling madness descend over her like a warm, invisible cloud as she turned and ran.

She lit out for the water, crouching down low in the early morning cold just in case. When she reached the beach, she turned left and headed south back towards Cabo San Lucas. She'd sprinted as long as she could, the crunch of the cold sand feeling good on her sore insteps. The muscles in her legs screamed as if she'd just run a marathon. She'd pushed herself harder than she'd ever dreamed but fear and adrenaline had kept her on her feet, moving forward in the direction of the hotel, back towards the safety of the real world. There were a series of crisscrossed tears in the normally smooth skin of her long legs from where she'd run through patches of untamed land, unconcerned about the ripping away of several layers of skin that now shrilly stung. She'd come across a small dirt road that she assumed led back to the highway just as the sun burst up over the horizon, the tall cacti casting long shadows that looked like sinister pitchforks in the dry dirt.

You're almost there, the voice crooned. *Soon this will all be a terrible memory. You'll go on talk shows and tell your story, maybe even sign a book deal. You'll be a celebrity, a hero just because you survived.*

The sound of an engine's roar brought her out of her stupor. They were coming for her. Her time was officially up. They'd discovered her absence and sent people to retrieve her. She turned around and saw the old black Nissan barreling down on her, a terrible but familiar face floating behind the wheel like a cartoon devil. She fell to her knees and raised her hands to her face as the vehicle came to a sliding halt inches from her head. She could feel the heat coming off the grill. A fresh wave of dread crashed over her.

Looks like it's too late now sweetheart, the voice said. *You had your chance and you blew it. Nice try but no cigar. See you on the other side kid.*

The car door opened, and Angel got out, smiling with relief at the sight of her.

"Buenos Dias Flaquita," he crowed. "We were starting to miss you."

Alexis devolved into a hysterical fit of tears. Her eyes burned as she cried, more out of frustration than fear. She was beyond fear in that moment, too exhausted to feel anything. She knew the end was close, that it was inescapable now, and she cried pitifully, snot running from her nose. She prayed that it would be quick and painless but knew that wasn't likely, not after she'd almost escaped. They were sure to punish her more for it. There was no way around that now.

Angel impatiently grabbed a fistful of her hair with his right hand, the stubby calloused fingers yanking until she let out an involuntary gasp. With his left hand he slapped her so hard she saw stars. Before she could open her mouth to speak he struck her over the head with something hard made of metal. There was a loud pop and she felt hot blood pour from the stinging wound in her cracked skull. She fell to the ground, her cheek burning against the hot dirt. A glossy, black scorpion came rushing up to greet her from underneath the shade of a nearby cactus. The last thing she saw before she passed out was Angel's dusty sneaker stomp down hard and crush it to death.

Chapter Six

Zack was feeling much more relaxed by the time they reached resort row and made their way out of Oscar's wonderfully chilled transportation into the tropical heat of Cabo. Dave had managed to get him to do three full shots of tequila between the airport and the hotel and he was becoming aware of a persistent nagging in his bladder. He realized he hadn't taken a piss since LAX about the same time as the liquor began to intensify the problem. He sprinted past Dave—who was busy doling out tip money to Oscar like Willy Wonka handing out sweets to children—and rushed into the lobby of the nearest hotel. He barely made it, rushing into the first available stall while fumbling with the zipper of his jeans and cursing in a buzzed stupor. He let out a low, deep moan of relief as the hot jet of urine came steaming out of him, forming tiny bubbles in the water below. Zack absentmindedly noticed that they resembled a series of interconnecting amber-tinted skulls that seemed to grow in exponential numbers by the second, until the whole bowl was practically filled with them.

Like something you'd see inside a catacomb, Zack pondered, *or a mass grave.*

A cold shiver ran down his spine at the morbid thought. Zack forced the image from his mind and flushed the toilet. He took his time washing his hands and face in the cool water from the sink, letting his nerves settle back down before heading outside. He was feeling like a million bucks by the time he jogged over to the curb again, the visceral sense of dread that had unexpectedly gripped him just moments before now completely forgotten. Oscar was long gone but Dave was standing next to their luggage. Zack hurried over and grabbed his bag, swinging it up and behind him.

"Where are we staying again?" Zack asked.

"Last one on the left," Dave said, trundling forward with his wheeled bag. Zack followed, enjoying the feeling of the gritty sand underneath his flip flops as it crunched against the hard stone road beneath.

"So why didn't we just have Oscar take us all the way up to the front of the place like normal people then?" Zack prodded.

"I never let anyone know where I am going if I can help it," Dave said, the paranoid look he usually had back at home returning full force to his buzzed face. "That's how you get robbed or held for ransom. Trust me. It happens a lot down here. It's practically a respectable occupation in places like Mexico City."

Zack nodded, realizing at last why Dave had made such a huge fuss with the customs official for demanding to know where he was staying. *Makes sense now that he didn't want to announce it to the entire line of strangers from the plane.*

"Okay," Zack said. "So why not hire security guards then? It's not like you can't afford it."

"Pass. That's a guaranteed way to make yourself a target. You might as well just announce you've got ransom money. Besides they'd just slow us down with the ladies," said Dave, wriggling his eyebrows for maximum effect.

Another thought struck Zack as they strolled along. He turned to his friend. "Remind me again how are you going to score drugs off that guy later if you won't let him know where you're staying?"

"That's easy," Dave explained. "We'll place the order in town. It's safer that way anyway. You never know who is listening in to your calls down here. Front desk clerks are known to sell information to local thugs in exchange for a cut of the action. That's why you never let them plan your vacation activities either. Everything you do should be last minute, totally unscheduled. Cuts down the chances of them picking up on your routine and lying in wait for you when you don't have one. Am I right?"

"Wow," Zack laughed, coming to a halt to stare in awe at his friend. "That settles it. You really are the most paranoid person I know."

"Sorry man. Old habits die hard. I'll dial it back. I promise," Dave said as a dark look flashed across his face. "It's just that when you've had people come after you for your money you start to second guess everyone you meet. It becomes like a defensive instinct. I don't even notice I'm doing it."

"It's cool man," Zack said dismissively, hoping to change the subject to something lighter. "We're on vacation now. Just try to relax and enjoy yourself."

They walked up the long driveway to the front of the five-star resort to find young men in fresh-pressed uniforms parking cars and helping guests carry their luggage. One of them tried grabbing Dave and Zack's bags but Dave waved him off.

"*No gracias mi amigo*," he said with an amused chuckle. "My bags stay with me."

I guess he's right, Zack thought. *Old habits do die hard.*

Near the front of the resort lobby they passed a parked police car with the trunk open. An older looking cop with a barrel chest and a thick black mustache was picking up a row of pink suitcases one at a time off the sidewalk and loading them into the back. He stopped and stared menacingly at Dave and Zack as they passed.

Inside the resort was a large aquarium in the lobby full of some of the most beautiful tropical fish Zack had ever seen. There was a row of brochures for everything from fishing expeditions to parasailing to the fabled booze cruise party boat. Zack flipped through them as Dave went to the front to check in. The concierge was a nervous little man with a name tag that read MIGUEL. He had bulging eyes and a receding hairline. He fidgeted nervously as he informed Dave that his room was still being cleaned. He asked Dave to wait in the lobby while the maids finished up.

"Have a seat over there," Miguel motioned towards Zack on the couch.

"How long is this going to take?" Dave asked, not bothering to hide his annoyance at having to wait.

"Not long," Miguel simpered with a practiced smile. "I promise you."

Dave sulked over to the sofas and plopped down next to the exotic tank, staring listlessly at an orange-and-blue striped Clarion Angelfish that had turned to watch him. Zack joined him, bringing along a handful of pamphlets for activities like bungee jumping and zip lining through the jungle canopy.

"This fish right here alone is worth over twenty-five hundred dollars back home," Dave said. "And that's if you can find one."

"Twenty-five hundred dollars for one fish?" Zack asked incredulously, his mouth hanging open in shock. "That's insane!"

"Exotic fish are no cheap hobby my friend," Dave said. "Some of them cost tens of thousands. This little fellow's from Mexico though. Down here they're probably a dime a dozen. It's once you try to get him out of the country that you get shafted."

Dave laid his head back and closed his eyes while Zack began to examine the swirling colors in the tank in earnest, wondering just how expensive the entire collection was. After a few moments the cop they'd seen out front came in, walking briskly to the front desk, the heels of his cowboy boots clicking steadily against the tile mosaic of the lobby floor. He stood in front of the check-in desk and cleared his throat to get Miguel's attention.

"*Lo siento,*" the concierge began. "I didn't see you there, Officer Reyes. I hope that you got everything you needed? That our little problem has been taken care of?"

"Would I be standing here if I had everything I needed?" the officer snapped.

Miguel nervously glanced around to make sure he wasn't being watched. The cop didn't budge an inch. Finally, Miguel reached beneath the desk and brought up a large envelope, sliding it across to the officer. He took it, quickly flipping through the contents before folding the envelope over and stuffing it in his pocket.

"I trust we won't have this happen here again," Miguel said condescendingly. "It's not good for our reputation."

"Who can say? Seems like it comes with the job these days.

Cost of doing business," Officer Reyes deadpanned.

"I pay a lot of money to avoid having this exact kind of problem and still…" Miguel's words trailed off as a couple of college kids in bathing suits walked by headed for the pool. "It can't happen again. That's all I'm saying. I'm under a lot of pressure."

"You don't know what real pressure is," Reyes snorted. "Try answering to the Commandante for everything that goes wrong in a town full of entitled American kids stoned out of their mind on drugs and alcohol while he's off sucking up to the Governor. Then you'll know what pressure is my friend."

"Guests can't just go missing," Miguel hissed. "If word got out about this it would kill our business!"

"*Exactamente*," the cop sang. "So, let's be clear, you pay me to clean up your messes, and for my discretion. Remember that. I'm not an errand boy that's going to jump every time you snap your fingers. I'm here as a favor to your boss, *entiendes*?"

"I've got a lot of work to finish if you don't mind," Miguel said dismissively, returning to his computer. "Go ahead and show yourself out."

The cop stood there in shocked silence for a moment before replying. "You ever talk like that to me again *pendajo* and I'll cut your tongue out and feed it to the *pinche* birds," he growled. "*Comprende*?"

Miguel visibly gulped, raising his head to make eye contact once more before nodding. The cop turned and stormed out passing Zack and Dave as he went. The phone rang, and Miguel nervously answered it, saying something quickly into the receiver before abruptly hanging up. He took a moment to recompose himself before calling out to them.

"Your room is now ready," Miguel said. Zack couldn't help but notice that the fake smile that seemed to stretch from one ear to the other on their arrival now looked like a half-deflated party balloon the morning after. Dave, on the other hand, was still totally oblivious.

"Grassy ass seen yor," Dave obnoxiously brayed, snatching the room keys from him and heading down the hall towards their room.

Chapter Seven

Wakey wakey, the voice deep inside of her taunted. *Time to pay the piper, Red.*

Alexis awoke to a series of sharp pains screaming through her body. She was naked now, kneeling on jagged concrete in front of a small altar, her knees bleeding, her arms twisted painfully behind her back and bound together with what felt like barbed wire. The more she struggled the deeper it cut into her soft skin. Her legs were bound in it as well, preventing her from trying to stand. She'd been exposed for some time from what she could tell. Her skin itched in places where the insects had bitten her, causing her to squirm. Her head pounded where she'd been bludgeoned, a searing migraine gripping her skull and making her grit her teeth in agony.

It's time to meet her in person, the voice squealed. *Saint Death.*

Her blurry vision cleared, causing the image of a blood covered statue to come into focus. It was just as Francois had described, a skeleton of a woman dressed in a wedding gown, wearing a gaudy bejeweled crown and adornments. In her right hand she held a scythe, like the grim reaper. In her left she held a globe. At her feet were several bowls, each filled with different illicit substances. There was one with dark, coagulated blood, another with a burning sprig of marijuana, and a third with what appeared to be a pile of snow-white powder she guessed was cocaine. In between these were stacks of money in different currencies and denominations, ranging from dollars to Euros to pesos. The last thing she saw on the altar was an old black leather Bible with gold lettering that read *Maria.*

Looking up she saw that the people from the night before who'd been dancing around wildly, beating drums and celebrating her impending death were now gone. The place was empty except for her abductors and their guest of honor.

Looks like you threw a monkey-wrench into their original plan with your little escape attempt, the voice cackled. *Got the place all to yourself now.*

She knew the high priestess was still there because she could hear the woman chanting loudly behind her as flecks of something wet and sticky hit her back. The sensation caused her to flinch, then wince in pain as the restraints bit into her. At last the evil woman appeared in front of her confirming her presence, the bright flowers of her elaborate woven headdress swaying in the ocean breeze, her face painted like a freshly bleached skull.

She is the living embodiment of the statue she worships, the voice explained. *The conduit between the supernatural and the mundane. She serves the darkness and feeds the unholy spirit the blood and suffering of her enemies.*

The high priestess held up a blood-smeared machete as she cruelly leered at Alexis. The guest of honor, a sweaty man with dark skin wearing cowboy boots and a straw hat, took it from her. His jeans were sun bleached a pale blue that matched the sky overhead. His teeth were capped in gold and he wore a dazzling assortment of gold-plated necklaces and rings to match. He stopped in front of her, his shiny golden belt buckle at eye level, the word SINALOA set in sparkling diamonds that brilliantly reflected the desert sun. She looked up to see that he had a checkered shirt on with B.O. stains under both pits. It was open to the middle of his chest where a tattoo of a big breasted woman with a skull for a face and roses for hair lewdly stared back at her. Amidst his gaudy display of wealth, he wore a simple rosary made of dark wood.

The man anxiously approached the altar, taking a handful of cocaine and rubbing it on the rumpled dress of the life-sized statue. He poured the blood onto the ground, mumbling in Spanish, then set the bowl between Alexis's legs. Alexis felt her bladder involuntarily let go in fear as hot rivulets of piss ran down her trembling inner thighs. The man with the gold teeth bowed his head and said what sounded like a short prayer, making the sign of the cross over himself before turning his attention back to Alexis. Nervously he grabbed her by her hair, yanking her head back painfully until the tears freely spilled down her face. Her heart raced as he chanted a series of dark incantations.

"Madre bendita" the man began, his voice quivering with earnestness, *"tú que estás más allá de toda forma, más allá del deseo, más allá del sufrimiento y la pérdida, concédeme tu poder y protección, para conquistar a mis enemigos y darme poder, riqueza y victoria total."*

Her mind raced, thinking back to the years of high school Spanish she had taken in an attempt to translate some of the words and make sense of what was happening to her.

Blessed mother, the voice translated for her. *That's who he is praying to, asking for protection from his enemies and to be free of all obstacles to success and power. He is worshipping death itself!*

A sadness began to overwhelm her as she realized these were to be her final moments. She had done her best to escape but the voice was right. She had failed.

It will all be over soon now, the voice in her head cooed. *All you can hope now is that he is quick about it, that the pain passes so we can both be at peace. Try not to think about it. That's a good girl. It's almost done.*

He slit her throat in one clean motion. The blood poured down the front of her. He grabbed her head as she kicked and thrashed and held the gushing wound over the bowl between her legs, collecting the bright scarlet fluid that poured out until it pooled over the sides. He dipped his finger in her blood and drew a cross on her forehead before shakily setting the bowl at the feet of Saint Death. He made the sign of the cross over himself, looking pale as milk, before turning and nodding to the high priestess. She nodded back with a generous smile, but he frowned in reply before heading back to his car as fast as his feet would carry him.

"Not everyone is a true believer," she said to Angel as she

watched the man go. She waited until he was in his truck, the engine revving as he pulled off and away from the killing grounds, before she spoke again. "We aren't finished yet."

"I know," Angel replied.

"The cartel specifically asked for enough sacrifices for each of their foot soldiers and enforcers," she angrily scolded. "They flew some of these men in from other parts of the country just for this. Esteban said that all of them must be baptized in blood before they go to war. He's very superstitious. Obviously, they have something big planned. You were supposed to round up just enough of them to satisfy their order without drawing extra attention to yourself. What happened?"

"Alajandro got greedy," Angel shrugged, his eyes still cast down. "It wasn't my fault."

"We're going to need to replace the one he killed," she informed him coldly.

"Isn't there someone here we can use instead? Maybe one of the new girls? I'll drag them out quietly, so I don't wake the others. We can say they ran away if anyone starts asking, that they got scared. What about that new girl who never speaks? Silvia? She'd be perfect," Angel offered, hoping to make an easy task of it.

"Absolutely not," Maria said looking shocked and appalled at the suggestion of sacrificing one of her followers.

"Why not?" Angel demanded. "Most of them would be honored to die for the holy Mother, if you told them it was what she'd commanded, and you know it!"

"You remember what happened last time a Santa Muerte sect used locals for blood magic? They were all arrested and carted off, but not before being paraded in front of the national news so all the journalists could interrogate them like savages then humiliate them for their beliefs in print," Maria said, a dark look falling over her visage like a widow's veil. "I will not have our dear Mother spoken ill of by intellectual snobs with no understanding of her powers. I would rather die first!"

"Calm down. Those were little kids," Angel argued. "I'm talking about a full-grown adult. If not one of ours then perhaps a local *puta* no one will miss?"

"That's exactly the kind of lazy thinking that gets people arrested and sent to prison," she replied.

"We don't need to worry," Angel said. "She will protect us from harm, from our enemies, right? That's what you tell us all the time. That's what you believe, isn't it? That Santa Muerte will punish those who oppose her followers and make us rich?"

"I suppose you're right," Maria relented, moved by his religious plea. "But that is no reason to get sloppy. Besides, the last sacrifice specifically needs to be a young man, preferably American."

"*¿Por qué?*" Angel asked.

"The final ritual we are performing is for the cartel's number one hit man," Maria explained. "Ramon has a taste for torture and will want to take his time, which is why we saved him for last. The others were all new to the cartel, new to the faith you could say, since they had no inclination of worshipping Santa Muerte before joining. Esteban makes them swear allegiance to the Bony Lady before sending them into battle. They believe they can determine how loyal a new recruit is by how willing they are to kill for their new boss, but on a deeper level they know the power this blood magic holds. Ramon began devoutly worshipping the Skinny One when he was just an enforcer for the Mexican Mafia. He claims he's been killed no less than three times but that our Great Mother Death has brought him back to exact revenge on his enemies. Some say he is now unkillable."

"So why does it have to be an American?" Angel demanded.

"He hates *Gringos*," Maria shrugged.

"Who doesn't?" Angel replied.

Angel began to walk past her, but she stopped him.

"We don't have a lot of time," she admonished. "The cycle of the moon will soon change, and the ritual will be less powerful. Ramon is already asking when we will be ready for him. He knows something is off. I can't hold him off forever."

"I will work fast," Angel promised.

"Good. And bring a replacement this time, in case there is another accident," Maria commanded.

"Not a problem," Angel reassured her.

"I don't want you to take any chances," Maria insisted.

"This needs to happen quickly and cleanly. This isn't just about money. Even though I've known Esteban for years there's no telling what he will do to us if we fail him. The reputation of his cartel depends on the appearance of strength, especially with the losses they've taken at the hands of Zetas in the last six months. Our lives may depend on this. Am I clear?"

"*Si madre,*" Angel said, turning away from her. "I won't let you down again."

"*Gracias miho,*" she said, gently patting him on the shoulder. Slowly he turned back to face her, tears welling up in his eyes. "That's a good boy."

Chapter Eight

The room had finally stopped spinning. Zack stood up again, feeling a little less disoriented than when he'd stumbled in. He was on a huge hotel bed with the glossy, lacquered blades of a handcrafted palapa ceiling fan wafting cool air conditioning down onto his slightly burned skinned. The sun had gone down outside but he was still wearing his shorts from earlier at the pool. He slowly padded to the bathroom of the palatial suite Dave had rented them for the week and threw up one last time for good measure.

Almost immediately after checking in they'd changed into trunks and hit the swim up bar, just as Zack had wanted. Zack was surprised his friend didn't offer any resistance or have another scheme hatched for them, but Dave just shrugged and said it would solve the problem of his flagging buzz.

"Plus, it will give us a chance to scope out the *lay of the land* so to speak," Dave added with a lecherous wink before grabbing them a pair of towels from the bathroom. "There should be a fair number of hot girls in tiny bikinis already either in the water or basking in the dirty Mexican sun by now. Time for this player to get down to business. I'm hoping to sleep with a new girl each night we're here. If I fail to hook up tonight I'll have to double up tomorrow, maybe grab a pair of hot twins. Don't get me wrong. I appreciate a challenge as much as the next man…"

"If the next man is Barney Stintson," Zack mumbled.

"But I also don't want to strain myself by overdoing it right out the gate. Let's just see if we can both ease into our respective grooves by flirting with a pair of pretty girls with low self-esteem to start out with. We'll see where things go from there.

Even the best athletes have to warm up and stretch before the big game."

Zack rolled his eyes but secretly he was happy not to have an argument. The pool was packed and, even though there were far more guys than girls, Dave seemed to be happy with the quality of the single ladies they met. He set his sights on a busty brunette from Akron named Serena, putting his best face on and cracking jokes until she laughed like a hyena with an overbite, only to discover she'd come with an overweight boyfriend who shied away from any activities that involved taking his shirt off. By the time her man came waddling over to collect her for their early dinner reservations Zack was so drunk he could barely stand up. He'd been helping himself to some sweet fruit concoction called a Yellow Bird courtesy of the amicable pool bartender Carlos and had lost count of how many he'd consumed. Dave had to help him back to their room. Zack threw up the entire contents of his stomach then passed out on his bed.

The nausea he'd felt earlier had passed after his last regurgitation, along with the intoxication, leaving a deep hunger in its place. Dave was watching the Dodgers play an early season game against the Arizona Diamondbacks but shut it off when Zack came into the room.

"There's my mad dog killer," Dave said, getting to his feet.

"If I never drink anything yellow again it will be too soon," Zack said, gingerly rubbing his temples.

"How's your head feeling?" Dave chuckled.

"Not as bad as I thought it would," Zack grinned. "You?"

"I'm a seasoned degenerate," Dave chuckled, slapping his belly. "The swim up bar was child's play for a primed liver like mine. Now I'm ready to do some serious drinking. What about you?"

"Not until I get something in me," Zack said. "Didn't you say this place had a buffet?"

"There are a few restaurants inside the resort, but you need a reservation for most of them," Dave said. "I put us down for the steakhouse tomorrow but tonight I thought we'd go out, catch some local culture, maybe grab a few street tacos before hitting the bars."

"You said we were going to stay here and see what the resort had to offer," Zack argued.

"And we did," Dave replied. "But in case you hadn't noticed all the single ladies started heading into town before the sun went down. This time of night the resort is mostly older married geezers in Tommy Bahama shirts trying to rekindle the spark or rich dudes with their mistresses getting couples massages on the lanai. If you want to meet girls our age, we're going to have to go into town sooner or later."

Zack eyed him suspiciously. "This isn't just a ploy to score dope is it?"

"What? No! Come on man," Dave answered growing defensive. "I just want to meet a nice girl or two that wants me to defile them in a way their boyfriend back home would never dream of, that's all!"

"Promise me this isn't going to turn into a disaster of a night if we go into town," Zack demanded.

"Scout's honor," Dave said, solemnly holding up his right hand with three fingers up and his thumb tacking down a curled pinkie in mock salute.

"I'm serious man," Zack insisted.

"Relax bro," Dave said nonchalantly. "What's the worst that can happen?"

"If we end up getting tossed in a Mexican jail because of you I swear I will never forgive you," Zack warned, but Dave blew it off with a chuckle.

"You're overthinking things again," Dave assured him. "Go change into something we can hit the clubs in after we get dinner, so we don't have to come back to the hotel. We'll meet back here in five."

Zack went back to his room and pulled out a pair of designer jeans, slipping into them before choosing a black button up shirt that wasn't too wrinkled. He pulled it on then did his best to smooth it out with his flat palms. For a finishing touch he sprayed on some cologne. He spotted his passport sticking up out of his bag when he went to zip it up. Remembering what Oscar had told them on the ride into town he picked it up and slid it into his front right pocket for safe keeping before leaving the room. Dave was already waiting for him, and full of zest.

"Look at this fancy bastard." Dave greeted him with a slap on the back. "Is that a hint of cologne I detect?"

"Stop busting my balls and let's go," Zack groused. "I'm starving."

"After you *Seeenyoooor*," Dave comically bellowed. Zack rolled his eyes as they headed out of the room for the night, locking the door behind them.

Chapter Nine

The evening had gone just about as Zack had expected. They'd walked up resort row towards the end before catching a cab, since Dave in his paranoia of being targeted for his money didn't want anyone to know where they were staying. Dave had struck up a polite if overly friendly conversation with an older couple from Detroit down for their honeymoon, then talked them into splitting cab fare over to the main part of town. They'd ended up settling on street tacos after all, at a bustling place filled with gringos. Local merchants wandered around the crowded tables, pitching their wares to largely disinterested tourists while a drunk old man with an acoustic guitar serenaded couples loudly and off key in Spanish. Dave and Zack got lucky enough to score a table near the street with a bird's eye view of the plaza.

While they ate, a skinny Mexican guy in his late twenties tried desperately to sell them a sack of weed but Zack just kept telling him no. When it became clear that they weren't going to budge the man then switched to asking for a small donation to help feed his family. Moved by the man's sad tale of needing heart surgery for his youngest son Zack reached into his pocket for a few pesos but Dave stopped him with a stern look. Eventually the man went on to harass another group of college kids at the end of the Taqueria's patio.

"What was that about?" Zack complained. "I was just going to give him a couple pesos to help him out."

"He doesn't have a sick kid," Dave said matter-of-factly.

"Probably not," Zack admitted, "but that doesn't mean he's not suffering. What would a few pesos hurt? I've seen you waste more on drinks for strangers."

"It's a set up," Dave said with a knowing smile. "I read about it online while you were napping."

"On what?" Zack asked flippantly. "Scams are us dot com?"

"There's a site some Americans who live down here put up to warn visitors," Dave said, folding up a *carne asada* taco and shoving the whole thing noisily into his mouth as he spoke. "I got to thinking about what Oscar had said and decided to see what other kinds of scams there were. The last thing I want is to spend more time in jail being harassed by Mexican cops for a payout. This was one of the main ones the site warned about."

"Go on," Zack said, his eyes watching as the anxious dealer accosted a longhaired surfer with a bad sunburn. The kid shook his head back and forth before reaching into his trunks and handing him a hundred-peso bill just to go away.

"First he tries to sell you drugs," Dave said with a snort. "That's an open and shut way for them to make a fast buck off you. If you don't buy up they begin begging for a donation, anything to help them out, but it's just part of the sting. The sign to move in is the exchange of money, which the police will say was him paying for drugs."

"That's insane," Zack argued. "Besides when they stop and search him they see he's clean. What good is shaking him down then?"

"Ah but that's the trick! He won't be," Dave said with a twinkle in his eyes. "They will pull him into their vehicle to search him on suspicion of buying drugs and they'll put a bag of pills or an eight ball of cocaine right in his pocket then pull it out in front of him. One guy said they had a paper sack already in the police cruiser with a full brick of heroin they said was his. That's when they start shaking you down for some good old American greenbacks!"

"Come on man," Zack laughed, "You're just being paranoid again. I mean how do they even know? Is the guy that just tried to sell us weed going to then rat out his customers to the police?"

"He doesn't have to," Zack said, reaching over and taking one of Zack's tacos, an al pastor with grilled pineapple on top of it. "They're already working together before he comes out to sell for the night. That's who gave him the weed no doubt.

Somewhere nearby in the crowd is an undercover watching the whole time. There. The guy in the black hat. Look but don't let him know you're looking."

Zack turned to see a man in a black coat and hat watching them from across the street. The man was standing with a newspaper open but not bothering to read it. On the cover were images of cut up bodies and lurid headlines about growing cartel violence. He locked eyes with Zack, who casually looked around as if he were taking in the scenery rather than singling him out. When he looked back again the man was intently watching the longhaired surfer again, who was receiving a wealth of praise and compliments from the man he'd just helped.

"The web site said they wait for the dealer to wander off before moving in," Dave explained. Zack looked back over to see the man stuffing the hundred-peso bill into his pocket and walking away. He glanced across the way to the man in the black hat, who was now excitedly talking on a cell phone. A moment later a police car pulled up and stopped next to the patio. Two officers got out and surrounded the surprised surfer kid, dragging him to the car and forcing him inside. The man with the black hat calmly walked over and got in the back with him.

"And so, it begins," Dave said, turning back to Zack, whose mouth was hanging open in shock at what he'd seen.

"That's insane," Zack said. "We've got to help him. He didn't do anything wrong." He started to get up but the look on Dave's face made him freeze in his tracks.

"There's nothing we can do for him man," Dave said. "If anything, we'd just make it worse. This is their world and we're just passing through it. To them we're all just a paycheck waiting to be tripped up and extorted. Trust me the police are the last people I'd go to for help down here."

"Which means if something goes wrong," Zack said, "we're on our own?"

"Pretty much," Dave said, finishing off Zack's last taco now that he'd lost his appetite. "Luckily most real trouble is easy to avoid if you know what to look for."

"Like over eager dealers?" Zack asked earnestly.

"Exactly," Dave said, standing up and leaving his pile of trash on the table. "So, tell me my dear old friend, how are you feeling now that you've gotten a couple tacos in you?"

"Good as new," Zack smiled weakly.

"Excellent," Dave said, turning his arms towards the long street already bustling with young college kids starting to party and get loud as they made their way in and out of the seemingly endless procession of local bars. "Adventure awaits us!"

Dave sauntered across the road towards the first bar where five girls in bikini tops and short skirts were lined up to get inside, his eyes glassed over like a kid in a candy store.

Zack cast one last look at the surfer in the police cruiser, who had his head down and was now crying. He felt a stab of guilt in his heart as he forced himself to look away. "Dave's right," he mumbled to himself. "All we can do is make it worse."

They spent the rest of the night in a blur of clubs, going from one to the next as Dave tried his best pick-up lines on group after group of increasingly disinterested coeds. When he failed to get the reaction he was looking for he decided he'd been going about things all wrong. "These girls aren't buying the standard spiel," he said, a desperate look in his eyes. "It's market saturation. There's just too many options down here."

"What can you do?" Zack slapped his friend on the back in a show of sympathy, but Dave wasn't placated by the gesture.

"We've got to change the odds," Dave said, a lightbulb going off over his head. "We've got to set ourselves apart from the rest of the crowd and I know just how."

Dave stormed out of the club and Zack followed in his wake. He crossed the street and headed down to one of the more upscale clubs with a long line of well-dressed guests waiting to get in. The bouncer looked annoyed as Dave strode purposefully towards the front of velvet ropes.

"We're at capacity," the bouncer said sternly, heading off Dave before he began.

"That's okay," Dave said, holding up a hundred-dollar bill. "We have a reservation."

"We don't take reservations," the bouncer sneered.

"Then make an exception," Dave said, adding another

hundred. The bouncer hesitated a moment before pocketing the bills. He lifted the rope and ushered Dave and Zack through without another word. Once they were in he let out a loud, distinctive whistle.

A moment later Angel came out of a building across the street and made his way over to him. *"Que pedo güey?"*

"I think I just found what you were looking for earlier," the bouncer said. "I've got a couple working girls already inside. They should be easy enough to spot, if you don't know them already."

"And your cut?" Angel asked.

"Just pay the girls," the bouncer said. "I'll get it out of them."

"Can they keep their mouths shut?" Angel fixed a deadly glare at him.

"My girls don't say shit to no one," the bouncer swore. "If they do you have my word I'll cut them up myself and send you their eye teeth."

"Gracias," Angel said before slipping into the club.

"De nada," the bouncer replied, closing the ropes behind him and smiling as he turned back to the growing line of eager American kids waiting to get inside. "Easiest money I've made in a long time," he chuckled to himself.

Inside the party raged as two DJ's dueled it out while a bevy of bikini clad beauties gyrated in a foam pit, their lithe bodies wriggling to the music as green laser lights strafed them from high above. Dave wasted no time locating a waitress who set them up at a private booth with bottle service. She poured them both shots of tequila before winking at Zack and walking away, her hips swerving lusciously from side to side as she went. Dave made a big show of watching her go, then let out a long wolf whistle.

"Did you see the ass on that one?" Dave asked rhetorically. "Sweet baby Jesus! Now that's what I call an onion, because it brings a tear to the eye just to look at. Get it?"

"You're so clever," Zack said derisively. "I'd say don't quit your day job but we both know you don't have one."

"She sure was into you," Dave said, ignoring the petty jab. "Did you see the way she was looking at you? Dear Lord. Like you were a steak fucking dinner and she'd been stranded on a desert island starving her whole life. Why don't women ever look at me like that?"

"I thought you didn't want to call attention to yourself," Zack said as he lifted the shot and slammed it back.

"Under normal circumstances I don't but desperate times call for desperate measures," Dave crooned, pouring him a fresh shot. "Besides, what good is having all the money in the world if you can't use it to impress hot chicks?"

They proceeded to get good and trashed over the next hour, but Dave never got any closer to landing any of the girls he set his sights on. He tried buying some of them drinks but gave up when the girls refused to take an alcoholic beverage from an obviously horny male stranger with questionable motives.

Can you blame them, thought Zack.

When the attempt to win the ladies over with free booze failed, Dave began introducing himself to girls on the dance floor as a secret agent in training with the CIA. He told them it was a matter of national security that they come to our reserved VIP booth and party with us. Some laughed at his bold approach but most of them simply ignored his advances, pulling together on the dance floor and closing him out, like a school of fish forming a bait ball to keep away predators.

"It's hopeless," Dave said, rejoining his friend at the booth. Zack, who had spent the better part of the night polishing off the bottle of silver Patron on the table, served them up another round.

"That's okay buddy," Zack consoled him, a warm feeling spreading through him as he slammed down a new shot. "You tried. There's always tomorrow. We live to play another day."

"How many of those have you had tonight?" Dave asked in amazement.

"I kinda lost count," Zack admitted. "Just trying to get your money's worth."

"Or trying to forget about Lily," Dave prodded, but Zack made a loud farting noise with his mouth. He winked at Dave.

"Lily who?" Zack replied sarcastically.

"All right man! That's the spirit," Dave roared. "And since

you've got your head on straight now I think you might like to know that hot Delta Nu from the plane has been staring at you from the bar for the last ten minutes."

Zack turned and looked. Dave was right. She was staring right at them. Their eyes locked and she smiled and waved, giving him an open invitation to join her.

"Well?" Dave said encouragingly. "What are you waiting for? She's waving you over! Go on man!"

"Here goes nothing," Zack slurred, clumsily getting to his feet and heading in her direction.

"You've got this," Dave shouted over the music. "Just play it cool."

Zack drunkenly weaved through a crowd of people, bumping into a busy waitress as he jumped out to reach the bar and knocking her tray full of drinks to the floor in a sickening clatter. She yelled at him in Spanish until he pointed back to Dave and told her to put it all on their tab. The Delta Nu, who was now in a short black dress with her hair slicked back and held in place with an orchid hair clip, laughed as he pulled himself up the bar.

"I like to make an entrance," he joked, feeling more than a little embarrassed.

"I see that," she giggled, barely able to contain herself. "First the airport incident and now this. You sure know how to cause a scene."

"First of all," Zack began, trying his best to sound confident and playful instead of drunk, "the airport incident was my friend Dave's fault. He's a magnet for drama if I'm being honest. As far as the waitress goes, well what can I say? I was distracted by a beautiful woman. No one can blame me for that. If anything, that makes this all your fault!"

She playfully punched him, but her face reddened at the compliment.

"I'm Jamie," she said, sticking her hand out. He took it in both of his and kissed it with a dramatic flair.

"Zack," he said with a flourish. "At your service."

"Nice to meet you Zack," she said, locking eyes with him and flashing him a sexy smile.

"So, what brings you to Cabo?" Zack slurred.

"Me and a few of my sorority sisters were looking to blow off some steam," she explained.

"I go to UCLA, but I don't think I've ever seen you on campus before," he prodded.

"That's because I don't go there," she laughed.

Zack wrinkled up his face. "But you were on the same plane as us?"

"We're from UCSB. We just flew out of Los Angeles," she explained. "I drove everyone down in my Pathfinder and left it in long term parking near LAX. Car barn I think it was called."

"Ah... Santa Barbara," he said, stretching out the words like they were a magic spell. "So where are your friends now?"

"Those lightweights went back to the hotel already," she complained. "We started drinking hard at dinner but most of them can't put it away like I can. I'm part Irish so. I wasn't quite ready to call it a night so soon, so I decided to stay out on my own. Looks like it payed off bumping into you though."

"That settles it then," Zack grinned. "You're joining us at the booth. There's no way I can let you just wander around on your own in good conscience."

"I thought you'd never ask," she sighed in relief. "Lead the way, sexy."

Zack took her by the hand and pulled her back through the pulsing dance floor to the other side of the bar. He was halfway to the booth when he noticed the two dark haired local girls on either side of Dave laughing at some story he was telling them. They all looked up when Zack and Jamie arrived.

"And this is who I was telling you about," Dave said by way of introduction. "This is my best friend Zack."

"Hey," Zack said, sliding into the booth. "This is Jamie. She's from UCSB."

"Hi Jamie. I'm Dave. Pleased to meet you."

"You're the one who got arrested at customs and managed to pop out of his handcuffs," Jamie said wryly. "That was some show you put on."

"Detained," Dave protested. "I was never actually arrested."

"It's still an impressive trick," Jamie said. "How'd you do it?"

"A real magician never reveals his secrets!" Dave roared.

"He broke his wrist skateboarding in front of my house when he was thirteen," Zack said. "I begged my dad to let me build a launch ramp, every day, for like a year. Eventually he gave in. First week I get the thing done this genius goes flying upside down off the thing and fucks himself all up."

"I was trying to do a flip," Dave grinned. "Instead I came down on my flat palm full force. I heard this weird crunching sound. When I looked down my hand was bent up at a weird angle, sitting on top of my arm. I totally freaked out!"

The girls all made a disgusted face.

"My dad was convinced your parents were going to sue him," Zack said. "It's all he talked about for months, how any minute we were going to be sued into the poor house and it would all be my fault. He made me scrap the ramp after that too."

"Maybe they should have sued you," Dave teased. "My wrist never did heal right."

"Think of all the bar bets you'd have lost," Zack shot back. "Ever seen then he's been able to pop it out of place. Handcuffs are all but useless on him. Cops hate it when he does it though. It freaks them out."

"All the more reason to mess with them," Dave said.

Jamie snuggled up to Zack, wrapping her tiny hands around his left arm like she was staking her claim on him as she suspiciously eyed the two other women. They laughed into their hands in reply as Dave poured them all a fresh round of shots from the now nearly empty bottle of tequila.

"Don't you worry now Jamie," Dave winked, sliding a fresh shot of Patron her way. "Both of these lovely ladies are already spoken for, at least for tonight."

The one to his right kissed his cheek in reply.

"This is Yesenia," he said. "She's got a lot of fire in her. And this is her friend Rosa. Rosa is dark and mysterious. She doesn't say much but she understands, isn't that right sweetheart?"

Rosa nodded as she glared at Jamie and Zack. Dave held up his shot and the others followed his example.

"Here's to making new friends in foreign countries," Dave

cried out like an auctioneer before slamming back his shot. Jamie gulped hers down like drinking water and poured another. Zack made a sick face as he did his best to get half of a shot down. Jamie threw back the second shot without noticing. Zack looked queasy but tried to smile through it.

"What's the matter?" Jamie asked. "You don't like tequila?"

"I'm not used to drinking so much of it at once, but I got this," Zack assured her, taking a couple deep breaths before slamming back the rest of his shot. His eyes watered as he triumphantly held up the empty glass. The girls all cheered in unison. Zack watched as Yesenia passed Dave a small brown bottle filled with white powder. Dave leaned down towards the table and put the bottle to his right nostril, taking a big hit of whatever was in it. A sick feeling shot through Zack. Dave seemed to sense it as he sat up, rubbing his nose and slyly passing the bottle back to Yesenia, who poured a little hit onto her long, bright red pinky nail and quickly sniffed it up.

She held the bottle out towards Zack and Jamie. "*Quieres?*"

Zack waved his hand, nervously looking around to make sure they weren't being watched. Jamie just laughed and reached for the bottle again. "I've got a nice buzz going," she said with a wink, pouring herself yet another shot. "I think I'll stick to the booze."

Jamie slammed back the third shot and sucked on a lime. Yesenia openly stared at her with a look of disdain but Jamie either didn't notice or simply didn't care. She climbed into Zack's lap and began making out with him in front of everyone. Zack couldn't believe his luck as the hot blonde sorority girl lost all inhibition and began to grope his chest and run her fingers through his hair. She tasted like citrus and alcohol but underneath that was a sweetness that reminded him of the first girl he'd ever kissed, Jackie Green, way back in junior high school. He could feel himself stiffening uncomfortably in his jeans. He gently pushed her back off him. Jamie resisted a little at first in her drunken state, but his embarrassment at pitching a tent in public eventually won out and she sat back staring dreamily at him for a while.

Rosa leaned over and whispered something fast in Spanish

to Yesenia, who quickly turned and began scanning the crowd for faces.

"What's wrong?" Zack nervously asked.

Yesenia quickly turned back and slunk down in the booth.

"*Policia*," Yesenia said, pointing behind them.

They looked out across the club to see the weed dealing snitch they'd encountered earlier at dinner talking to the bartender. He had a photo in his hands. He was looking for someone.

"Hey," Dave said, perking up. "I recognize that guy. He tried to sell us weed."

"He was working for the cops," Zack said. "He set up a surfer kid who gave him some change."

"He's a bad man," Yesenia said at last. "*Peligroso*. Dangerous."

Rosa looked frantic. She ducked down and spoke rapidly again in a blur of fiercely whispered Spanish.

"What is she saying?" Jamie slurred.

"We're not safe," Yesenia said. "We need to go. Follow me."

"Follow you where?" Dave asked.

"There is a house nearby we can party at," Yesenia said. "My friend owns it."

"I don't know about that baby," Dave said, shaking his head violently back and forth. "It's never a smart idea to wander off the reservation with two ladies you just met."

Yesenia took him by the face and turned him towards her.

"I've got more blow at the house," she purred. "Besides, don't you want to go somewhere that we can be all alone?" Before he could answer she stood up and put her breasts in his face. Zack didn't have to wait to see the expression on his friends face to know he was a lost cause. Dave sprang up from the booth, grabbing Yesenia by the hand.

"All right then you've made a believer out of me," Dave said eagerly. "Let's go!"

Yesenia turned back to Zack. "You can bring your little friend with you if you want," she said, a malicious glint in her eyes.

"Good," Jamie said, taking one last shot and polishing off the bottle. "Because I wasn't planning on letting this one out of my sight any time soon." She kissed Zack once more with tongue before climbing back to her feet.

Yesenia lead them through the crowded club and into the off limits empty kitchen area. Rosa was waiting by a side door smoking a cigarette. She ushered them out and into the dark, hot night. They stumbled along for a while, walking behind the clubs, the silhouettes of unseen strangers dancing around them in the shadows like demons let out of hell to play on Halloween night.

"Where are we going?" Dave asked as they scurried along in the darkness.

Yesenia stopped and pointed towards the brightest star in the sky. "There," she said, using her finger to draw a line straight down from the sky to a small house up on the hill with a light on. "That's where we are going."

Chapter Ten

When they came to the end of the alley Yesenia pulled them into an old, burgundy Toyota with an off-white hood, pulling out a baby seat and teething toys and throwing them in the trunk. They piled in and Yesenia cranked the ignition. The engine roared to life, followed by a loud backfire as the car stalled out. Yesenia cursed in Spanish through gritted teeth as she tried again, finally getting the car started up after several attempts and headed away from the clubs and neon lights.

"Are you sure this thing will get us there?" Jamie asked, making a face at Zack. "It feels like it's about to come apart at any moment."

"There's nothing wrong with the car," Yesenia shot back, her eyes narrowing to angry slits. "It just needs a little patience. We're not all lucky enough to buy brand new things whenever we feel like it."

"Sorry," Jamie said, holding her hands up in a peace gesture. "I didn't mean anything by it."

They drove the rest of the way in silence, passing through a small commercial area with closed shops. At the end of the street Yesenia swerved around a shirtless fisherman walking with a bucket and a rod and turned up an unpaved road towards the houses on the top of the small hill overlooking the sprawl of the Pacific Ocean. About half way up the road was blocked by a pack of wild dogs.

They look like they've been sewn together from a bunch of mongrel breeds, thought Zack as he watched them fight over a crow's carcass. *Like some kind of mutant dog version of Frankenstein's monster brought to life by some diabolical genius.*

Yesenia laid on the car's horn as a warning then revved the engine and shot straight at them. The feral beasts scurried out of harm's way as the car sped past, kicking up a cloud of dirt that rose against the clear night sky to ring the moon.

Jamie opened her mouth to speak but Zack beat her to the punch. "Don't say anything," he whispered in her ear, do his best to head off a fight between the girls.

A few moments later they pulled into the long white driveway of a ranch style house with a shimmering pool and walls made of glass facing the water. Yesenia led them inside single file and turned on the lights, giving them their first view of the expensive residence. The interior was decorated with plush white rugs thrown over Spanish tile. A series of sofas broke up the flow of the house with an open kitchen and attached wet bar off to the left and a narrow hallway down to the right that presumably led back to the master bedroom. There were flat television screens on each of the clean white walls. There were also photos of beautiful, naked women posed on tropical beaches looking aroused.

Jamie dragged Zack to the window to look out over the infinity pool towards the ocean, but Dave couldn't help but inspect the pictures on the walls instead.

"Who did you say this place belongs to?" he asked.

"My photographer friend, Señor Clive," Yesenia rattled off. "He used to tour with Led Zeppelin and the Rolling Stones when he was younger, as a rock journalist. When he got older he switched over to shooting erotica because it pays better."

"Judging from the looks of this place I'd say it pays very well," Jamie said. "So where is he now?"

"He lives in Scotland and travels for work most of the year," Yesenia said, trying to hide the annoyance in her voice.

Dave held up a black and white framed photo of an older guy with spiky white hair. He had a big grin painted on his tan face and an even bigger Cuban cigar sticking out of his clenched teeth. Around his wrist was a solid loop of silver.

"And he won't mind us partying here?" Dave asked.

"He lets me stay here whenever I want, Yesenia explained. "We have an arrangement."

Rosa laughed, and Yesenia shot a dirty look at her.

"Interesting," Dave said, setting the photo back down.

Rosa made her way into the open kitchen and pulled several bottles of alcohol from the cabinet, setting them on the counter. She filled the blender with ice from the freezer and set to work on making her concoction. Jamie watched with interest as Rosa carefully measured out several shots of tequila before dumping them over the shiny blades. A loud hiss pierced the air as she opened a bottle of ginger ale and dumped it in as well. For a final touch she slashed open three limes and squeezed their juicy pulps into the mix, discarding their sticky, desecrated hulks on the counter and absentmindedly sucking her fingers.

"Go ahead and make mine a double sweetheart," Jamie prodded. "I've got a strong tolerance."

Rosa simply smirked at Yesenia, as if they were sharing an inside joke, then went back to work. The blender roared to life, drowning out the sound of everything else. When she was satisfied with the results Rosa poured the drinks into blue-rimmed glasses. Yesenia rushed to the kitchen to help Rosa, blocking the others view as she dumped a healthy dose of white powder over the top of each and quickly stirred it in. Angel had told her all she would need was a small amount, but she didn't want to take any chances. Rosa watched as Yesenia served up the tainted drinks to Jamie, Zack, and Dave, then poured two clean glasses for them. Jamie didn't waste any time taking a big gulp. From the look on her face Zack realized it was tarter than she'd expected.

"What's in this thing?" Dave said with a puckered expression still on his face. "It's so sore."

Rosa just smiled in reply as she sipped her drink.

"It's called an El Diablo," Yesenia laughed, taking her glass from Rosa and finishing it in a single gulp. "Tequila, lime juice, and ginger ale. It's best when the limes are freshly squeezed."

"I putting in extra juices for you," Rosa said in bad English, winking at Jamie.

"I appreciate that," Jamie slurred, swaying from side to side. Zack grabbed her and held her up as she let out a giggle.

"It's her favorite drink," Yesenia confided. "Go on. Tell her what you think."

Zack took a big swig and winced. The tartness of the lime juice faded leaving a strangely medicinal aftertaste. For a moment the distinct possibility that they were being drugged raced through his mind, but it seemed too far-fetched and he laughed it off. *You're getting as bad as Dave*, he thought, pushing his fears out of his head and finishing the frozen drink.

"Do you like it?" Rosa asked, the shyness giving way as a devious smile crossed her face.

Zack began to reply but found to his surprise that in addition to his lips and tongue not working his legs were giving out. He sat down comically on the floor, one finger pointing up in the air as he tried to speak. "Tsiiitspreeeeeetysssstrooooong," he managed, his words slurring together into an incomprehensible garble.

Jamie reached down to help him up, but Zack pulled her down towards him. She came crashing down on him in a tumble, letting out a loud cackle as she did. Zack fought with his unresponsive arms and legs to roll her off him and by the time she was laying on her back she was out cold snoring. The room lurched around his head without warning. Suddenly he couldn't keep his eyes open. He laid his face on the cold tile and tried to focus on his breath as the darkness came reaching up for him like a welcome stranger.

"You guys are just pitiful," Dave chided, slamming back the rest of his drink and setting the glass on the counter. He looked pleasantly lit up, his cheeks blazing red with alcohol, his eyes unfocused, the hint of a smile threatening to blossom on his relaxed face. "You need to learn to handle your booze better. Phfff. Amateurs."

"Come on baby," Yesenia said, taking him by the arm and leading him towards the large sofa.

"Where are we going, *mamacita*?" Dave slurred, as he stumbled along with her.

"I thought we'd give you a little show before we got down to business," Yesenia teased. She kissed Dave on the lips. Rosa brought him a fresh drink. Yesenia held it to his lips and made sure he drank, tipping the glass back until it was empty.

"It's cold," Dave complained. "But strong. I like it."

"There you go," Yesenia purred. "Now sit back and get comfortable stud and let us do all the work."

Dave slid back on the couch and began to unbutton his pants. Yesenia took off her shirt exposing her full breasts. Rosa leaned over, taking one in her hand, and sensually licked at her nipple. Yesenia let out a sexy fake moan that brought Dave to full attention. She pulled Rosa up into a sloppy kiss, their slick tongues darting sensually over one another. She was just starting to take off her pants when Dave began to loudly snore. Yesenia pushed Rosa away in disgust and pulled her shirt back on. Rosa looked hurt as she watched her friend walk back to the kitchen counter, take her cellphone out of her purse, and dial a number.

"It's done," Yesenia announced, walking back over and nudging Zack with her foot on his thigh. A rivulet of drool escaped the corner of his mouth, but he didn't stir. "Come on up and get them."

Ten minutes passed before there was a loud knock on the door. Yesenia opened it and Angel and Hector walked in carrying two extra-large, handmade blankets.

"Who is the girl?"

"She's no one," Yesenia quickly said. "We couldn't get her to leave so she's part of it now."

"*Puta*," Rosa spat.

Angel inspected Dave. "Are you sure he's still alive?" He said, turning his face back and forth in his hands.

"He has a high tolerance for drugs," Yesenia explained. "He'll live."

"You better hope he does," Angel smirked. "Or you'll have to answer to Maria."

"You said you wanted two," Yesenia complained. "We got you two. Now pay us our fucking money."

"Hold your horses," Angel sneered. "You'll get what's coming to you when we're finished here."

He signaled to Hector who brought over one of the colorful blankets and unfolded it next to the couch. Angel took a leather strap from his pocket and wound it around Dave's wrists, binding them quickly together like a cowboy hog tying a calf at a rodeo. When he was done he motioned to Hector and together they lifted Dave up and laid him in the middle of the blanket before casually rolling him up in it. When he was no longer visible they picked up either side and carried him outside to the open back of their car. They set the unconscious body inside and headed back into the house.

Wrapping Zack up in the blanket was easier, since all they had to do was roll him over onto it. Angel bound his hands as well with another leather strap. The whole process was over in less than five minutes, with both boys tucked snugly away in the belly of the car. Angel closed the trunk and began to walk towards the driver's side door, but Yesenia grabbed his arms and yanked him back. He took a wad of pesos out of his pocket and threw it at her feet. Yesenia scrambled to pick them all up as Hector and Angel got into their car to leave.

"What about the girl?" Yesenia pleaded.

"I didn't ask for a girl," Angel said coldly. "She's your problem now. Take care of her or I will come back and take care of you. *Adios.*"

Angel sped off. Yesenia fumed as she watched the bright red tail lights of the car grow smaller and smaller as he got further away. She paced back and forth pensively for a while before turning to Rosa. "What are we going to do? I've never killed anyone before."

"There's no need to kill her," Rosa said comfortingly. "She's a drunk. She'll never remember."

"I wish you were right. We can't just leave her here," Yesenia protested. "You don't know these people like I do. No one messes with them. They kill people for fun."

"I'll do it then," Rosa said, running her fingers through Yesenia's hair. "I'll cut her throat while she's passed out. She'll never even know what happened."

"You'd do that for me baby?" Yesenia said softly.

Rosa turned without another word and headed back into the house, ready to take matters into her own hands.

"We can't do it here," Yesenia called out behind her, but Rosa froze in her tracks. On the floor was an orchid hair clip and nothing more, the only sign that Jamie had ever been there.

"Where'd she go?" Rosa shrieked, her voice rising in fear. "She was just right here!"

"She's gone," Yesenia said, "which means we are fucked. Come on! Let's find her. She couldn't have gotten far."

"Or we could just run away," Rosa suggested, biting her lower lip. "We've got the money. We could always start over somewhere new."

Yesenia's eyes flashed with anger. "You know that's not possible!"

"Why not?" Rosa asked.

"Because I have a kid now," Yesenia yelled back at her in exasperation. "I have to think about my little girl first. You know that!"

"So, you bring her with us," Rosa cajoled. "We can make a fresh start."

"Where would we go?" Yesenia asked, ready to wind herself up for a fight but Rosa stopped her with an unexpected kiss.

"Anywhere you want *Mami*," Rosa said at last. "I don't care where I live as long as I am with you."

Chapter Eleven

Jamie couldn't feel her face as she trudged down the side of the hill and back onto the main dirt road that led to town. She knew something was wrong when she came to and saw two scary looking Mexican guys covered in tattoos from head to toe roll Zack up in a blanket and carry him out of the house. She'd managed to crawl to the patio door and slip out, closing it behind her. The canopy of stars overhead looked like a psychedelic version of Van Gogh's Starry Night with the drugs in her system, alive and moving like spiders crawling over each other on a great big ever-rotating platter.

She heard voices arguing in the front yard then saw the tail lights of a car heading away from the house and down the dirt road. She knew she didn't have much time. Soon they'd be back for her, but she wouldn't be there. She forced herself to her feet, crawling at first before clumsily standing upright and plodding forward like the rising dead. She'd been drinking hard since she was thirteen and her parents got divorced. Still no matter how bombed she got she was always able to function. The other girls at her sorority house had learned her little secret during pledge week and began playing games with her. Since then they'd come to rely on it to make sure they all got home in one piece on nights they went out binge drinking.

Say what you will about me, Jamie thought as she worked her way up and over the low wall by the infinity pool. *I may be an alcoholic but at least I'm reliable.*

She began working her way downhill like the seasoned drunk she was, comically stumbling along in the near dark. In the distance she could hear the wild dogs howling but she paid them no mind. She would have to take things one step at a time. *Right now, she told herself, you've just got to make it back down this hill and find help. Worry about everything else when and if it happens.* It was a creed that had served her well, particularly in difficult situations. It had helped her survive over the years, even kept her from being gang raped at a Frat party over the previous summer. It would work now. It had to. There was no other choice. She was flat out of options.

She reached the bottom of the hill and looked back. The lights were now turned off in the house and a car with headlights pointing in two different directions was racing down the unpaved dirt road in her direction. They were bound to see her if she didn't do something. Panic overtook her at the thought of being captured. Jamie turned to run but tripped over her feet clumsily and, flailing around with her arms making wide circles, came crashing down in a weed riddled patch of dirt by the side of the road. There was a biting pain in her side and she wondered for a moment if she was bleeding, too scared to check or even breath.

What if they see me? What do I do if the car stops and they get out? I'll fight. I'll kick and scratch and bite if I have to, even if they have a gun! I'm not letting anyone wrap me up and put me in the trunk!

She laid there catching her breath, her heart beating so loud she could hear the blood in her ears, as the car sped past. The windows were down, and she could hear the girls arguing with each other inside.

They didn't see me, she realized, relief flooding through her.

She rolled over and peered through a break in the scrub brush to see the red tail lights of the Toyota speeding away. She felt like crying but instead she let out a little victory laugh. They'd given up and fled the scene of the crime. All she had to do was make it back to her hotel and she could put this all behind her. No one would ever even know how close she'd come to being kidnapped and killed. She could fly back home later in the day, switch her ticket, and be back in her own bed in less than twenty-four hours if all went well, safe and sound.

"All I wanna do is climb under the covers right now and fall asleep," she said to the evening sky, tilting her head back to take it in once more.

It was the thought of curling up under her fluffy pink comforter with her plush robe on and her black cat George purring in her lap that finally brought tears to her eyes. More than anything she wanted to be able to just go home and forget any of this had ever happened. Then she thought of Zack's slack face as they bundled him up in old blankets and carried him off like a corpse and the whole fantasy of fleeing came crashing down around her like jagged pieces of glass.

No, she thought, her mind still feeling clouded by the drug she'd been slipped. *It isn't right. I've got to do something. I've got to tell someone what happened. I can't let them get away with this!*

Anger surged through her, burning off the sluggishness. She used it to give her the strength she needed to get back on her feet. She stumbled on as fast as her legs would carry her, the fire in her belly giving her new resolve and clarity despite having her head wrapped in a pharmaceutical cloud. She was going to make it right if this was the last thing she did. Off in the distance she could see the lights of the club zone where everything had started, the sound of the night's revelry coming in snippets as the strong onshore ocean breeze blew dust and sand in her face. She stumbled towards it one furious step at a time.

Chapter Twelve

The first rays of the rising sun were already transforming the icy darkness of night to a pale shade of blue as Maria kneeled before the blood splattered statue of Santa Muerte. She humbly bowed her head, lacing her fingers together tightly in supplication as she earnestly whispered her desperate prayer.

"Dearest Mother, great protector, I beseech you in my time of need. Our time is running out and your children need your help. Please, kind Mother, bring to us a worthy sacrifice that will appease our benefactors and bring them victory in battle. Look down on us your humble children with mercy and give us your comfort and aid now when we need it most. You who have conquered death and are beyond all morality alone understand our hearts, our ambitions, our need for blood."

Maria made the sign of the cross over herself before plunging into the more traditional prayers.

"Holy Mother, please grant me your favor. Bless me to overcome all difficulties so that for me nothing is impossible, and no obstacles or barriers can stop me. Bless me so that no enemies can defeat me, and no man can cause me any harm. Make me victorious in all my dealings and in everything that I do. Watch over us as your children and fill our house with wealth and power for all of our days by virtue of your protection. Amen."

Maria heard an approaching car as she began to rise, her eyes locked on the skull face of Saint Death.

"Thank you, Mother, who works swiftly to help her worshippers," Maria said before leaning over and kissing the bony face of the deity. She turned and watched as Angel and

Hector popped the trunk and wrangled the first unconscious body from it. Both men cursed under their breath as they brought the sleeping victim to Maria and laid him at her feet. She leaned over and stroked the tuft of disheveled brown hair from his face.

"Just the one?" she asked.

Hector and Angel were already jogging back to the car and lugging a second, almost identical looking boy from the car. They deposited him next to his friend.

"*Mida*. Two American boys," Angel announced, obviously proud of himself. "Just as you requested."

"And no one saw you with them?" Maria asked sternly.

"No mother," Angel replied. "I hired a couple of whores to lure them to another location and drug them. They left one of the nightclubs through the back alley and vanished into the night. Once they were knocked out we picked them up and brought them straight here. There is no way to trace it back to us. If anyone starts asking about them, they will run into a dead-end chasing after the hookers."

"When this is over I want you to track down the women you hired and kill both of them," Maria ordered. "Make it look like an angry customer if you can, but no matter what, make sure they're both dead. I don't want anything loose ends."

"You worry too much," Angel scoffed.

"And you don't worry enough," Maria snapped.

Maria gingerly put her right foot on Dave's face and rocked it back and forth. His mouth opened slightly, and drool ran out. His eyes flickered back and forth but he didn't wake.

"How much did those *putas* give them?" she asked.

"I told them to give each one just enough to keep them sedated for the ride," Angel said. "They should be fully awake again in the next few hours."

"I hope so for your sake," Maria said, her face growing dark, the thin lines around her lips sharpening as she frowned. "Our last client will want his victim to be wide awake as he tortures him. If they overdose and die you are taking his place."

An angry look flashed across Angel's face momentarily, as if he was considering bashing his mother's brains in on the sacrificial alter. Just as quickly as it had come it passed. Angel shook his head and laughed.

"*Vamos*," he said to Hector, shaking his head in disbelief.

Maria went back to praying in front of the blood stained alter as Angel and Hector dragged Dave and Zack across the yard towards the barn.

Chapter Thirteen

Officer Reyes sat fuming behind his desk. Over the years he'd taken a lot of abuse from his superiors, but nothing came close to the ration of shit he'd just gotten from his Commandante when he was called into his office for an early morning meeting.

"I'm sorry about the hour but it's the only time I've got this week," the Commandante started off.

"It's fine Commandante," Reyes assured him. "What's on your mind?"

"The reason I wanted to see you in person was to talk about the new recruits, and why we're having so much trouble with them," the Commandante continued.

Reyes knew what was coming next. In the last few weeks the Commandante had gone on a hiring spree, adding almost a dozen new officers to their roster. Instead of the usual training these men had been assigned to other officers to learn on the job. The results were nothing short of catastrophic, with seasoned officers teaching new guys every trick in the book when it came to extorting both visitors and locals alike. In some cases, vendors were being hit up for a small bribe by one pair of cops in the morning then another set in the afternoon or evening. The brilliant plan to arm and set these guys loose on the town had come from the Commandante himself, but now that it was falling apart he was shifting the blame back onto Reyes, as if it had been his idea all along.

Typical, Reyes thought, smirking to himself as the anger smoldered in his chest. *No wonder he's doing so well in politics. He's an expert at dodging blame and passing the buck.*

"I hate to come down on you like this, but the fact of the

matter is that you just aren't doing enough to train them," his portly superior insisted, slapping a thick folder down in front of Reyes to add insult to injury. "I've been getting a lot of complaints from residents and angry calls from *los Estados Unidos*. I've got my hands full with the Governor's re-election. I am counting on you to keep things flowing. I hope my trust and faith in you is not misguided."

"No sir," Reyes swiftly replied. "I'll take care of it."

"You better," the Commandante growled. "Otherwise you're going to be out there looking for a job with the rest of these losers. Do I make myself clear?"

"Yes sir," Reyes barked back, swallowing down his growing anger.

"Did you bring the money with you?" the Commandante asked, expectantly.

Reyes suspected the hand off was the real reason he'd been called in to this secret, pre-dawn rendezvous. He knew the Commandante was set to meet the Governor at a power breakfast with a group of city leaders and land developers in the next hour. He took a fat envelope full of pesos from his pocket and slid it across the desk. The Commandante quickly tucked the envelope into his suit jacket without checking it.

"Don't worry. It's all there," Reyes said derisively, "just in case you're wondering."

"Good," the Commandante replied. "When this is all over we will talk about your promotion, that is if you haven't burned this place to the ground by then. There are going to be a lot of doors opening up after the Governor is re-elected, a lot of opportunities to change your stars if you know how to be smart and play ball."

The Commandante patted him on the shoulder as he left and Reyes, despite hating being touched, did his best not to flinch. When he was sure his boss had left the building, Reyes got up and punched the file cabinet as hard as he could several times with both fists, causing slivers of pain to shoot up his arms.

"I would cut his pig throat and take the money back," Reyes mused darkly, "if I could just figure out how to blame it on someone else."

"Excuse me," a voice called from behind him. Reyes turned around surprised to see a young American girl with dishwater hair in a black dress staring at him, her dark pupils the size of saucers.

"Can I help you?" Reyes asked.

"I hope so," she said, wobbling back and forth like a drunk. "It's my friends. They were abducted."

"When?" he asked.

"Just a few hours ago," Jamie said, trying not to vomit.

"You'll have to file a missing person's report with one of my officers," Reyes scolded her. "I don't have time for this right now."

"No, you don't understand," Jamie argued. "They took us to this house on the hill and drugged us. They rolled my friends up in a blanket and carried them off. I barely managed to escape! You've got to do something. I think they're in real trouble."

"Have you been doing drugs?" Reyes narrowed his eyes and cast a judgmental glare at her.

"No! Please. Listen to me. They put something in our drinks," Jamie insisted. "Right before the guys showed up and kidnapped my friends. You have to do something!"

"Do you remember what these men looked like?" Reyes asked.

"Just the one with the tattoos," Jamie admitted. "I never got a good look at the other guy but the one in charge, he had two eyes drawn on the back of his head and the words ALWAYS WATCHING. And the girls who lured us back to the house— Yesenia and Rosa, if those were their real names, I'm not sure— were afraid of him. I could tell that much. That's why you've got to help me find them. I think something awful is going to happen if we don't find them. I've got a really bad feeling about it."

Reyes stared at her for a moment, as if he were considering the validity of her story. "Can you identify him if you see him again?"

"I believe I can," Jamie said confidently. She was still green around the gills but could feel her spirits starting to raise a little now that she was finally being taken seriously by someone in a position of authority. She'd spent the better part of the last hour arguing with the man at the front desk before being sent back to see the man in charge. Officer Reyes pulled the top of his file cabinet open pulled out a new folder. He thumbed through several mug shots then pulled one out and held it up in front of Jamie. Angel scowled at her from the glossy black and white photo.

"Is this the man you're talking about?" Reyes asked.

Jamie's eyes immediately lit up when she saw him.

"Yes! That's him!" She pointed wildly at the picture with her finger. "I'd know those eyes anywhere."

"I have an idea where they might have taken them," Reyes said with a frown. He grabbed his car keys off the desk and hurried towards the door. "There's a religious compound just outside of town that is rumored to practice black magic on unwilling participants. That man you identified is associated with them. We'll have to move fast if you want to see your friends alive again. Come with me."

"Wait," Jamie said, following behind him like a lost puppy. "Where are we going?"

"North," Officer Reyes replied without looking back. "Let's just hope we can get there in time."

Chapter Fourteen

Zack's head was ringing and his back hurt. He opened his eyes, but his vision was blurry and wouldn't adjust to wherever he was. He sat up, realizing as he did that his hands were bound together. He stared down at them, the pain in his temples throbbing, his throat dry and sore. He tried to remember where he was or how he had gotten there, but his head felt fuzzy. Slowly his eyes began to adjust, and he saw that his hands were tied together with leather straps. He was sitting on the cool floor of an empty barn in what appeared to be some sort of makeshift jail cell. He heard a low groan and turned to see Dave was in the cell with him, his hands bound together too.

"Ouch, my fucking head," Dave said, sitting up and doing his best to rub his face with his restrained hands.

"Dave? Oh, thank God man. I thought I was alone here for a minute," Zack said, his voice sounding scratchy and raw.

"What the fuck happened?" Dave asked, still trying to collect himself. "The last thing I remember I was about to get it on with two hot lesbians."

"I think we were drugged," Zack said, frantically looking around the darkened barn.

"What are you looking for?" asked Dave.

"Jamie," Zack said. "I don't see her. Maybe she got away."

"Yeah and maybe she was in on it," Dave huffed. "You ever think about that?"

"In on what man?" Zack fired back.

"Whatever the fuck this creepy shit happening to us right now is," Dave said. "Is that blood on the floor? Jesus fucking Christ man. What the fuck is going on?"

"Whatever it is I got a really bad feeling about it," Zack said.
"Me too," said Dave.

"I'm serious man," Zack said frantically. "I don't mean to sound like a coward but I'm scared shitless right now. This shit is freaking me the fuck out. What the fuck is going on?"

"Hold up," Dave whispered as the barn door swung open and light flooded in from outside. "Someone is coming."

"Good," Zack whispered back. "Maybe we'll get some answers."

"Just be ready to fight the minute they open the cell door," Dave hissed. "We may only get one shot at this so watch for my lead then just swing for your life!"

Angel and Hector walked confidently up to their cell like construction buddies happy to be finishing a tough job and ready to party all weekend.

"You *putos* ready to meet your maker?" Angel asked as he unlocked the cell door and stepped inside.

"You're making a big mistake," Dave started but Angel cut him off.

"No *pendajo*," he laughed. "You made the mistake, trusting those whores. And now you're going to pay with your life."

"I've got money," Dave said quickly, changing tactics. "Lots of money. I can pay you. Please. Just tell me how much you want to let me and my friend go."

"We don't want your money *Guerro*," Angel glowered. "*Quien con el diablo haya de comer, larga cuchara ha menester.*"

Dave and Zack turned to each other, their faces both gone sallow and white as the realization that their impending death was likely just moments away. All the plans they'd just made to overpower their captors seemed to vanish at once, like vapor rising in the heat of the morning sun.

Zack felt his lips trembling as he began to babble. "You don't have to do this," he argued, his brain desperately searching for a way out of the impossible situation he'd found himself in as Angel lifted him to his feet. "Seriously. If you let us go, we'll run away and never tell anyone. I swear."

"*Callate guey*," Angel said, backhanding Zack so hard across the face that he saw stars and both his ears rang. The pain was extraordinary and the fear coursing through his veins seemed to amplify it. He looked over in horror at Hector who was having a hard time getting Dave on his feet. Hector yanked Dave up again and again, but each time Dave refused to remain standing. Although he'd gone mute he was far from done fighting and clearly had no intention of helping his murderous kidnappers' dispose of him. Hector leaned over and delivered a sharp rabbit punch to Dave's kidneys. The clouded look of confusion and fear he'd had before burned away as white-hot anger rose up in his eyes. Dave glared at Hector, who held him firmly by the hands and yanked once more. He kicked at Hector's legs, hitting him in the shins and causing him to wince and curse and jump up and down in howling pain. Hector angrily drew a buck knife from his jeans pocket and turned on Dave, but Angel called out to him.

"No! They'll kill us all *culero*. Just drag him by the hair if you have to!"

Hector grabbed a handful of Dave's hair and began yanking him along. Dave screamed in pain. His hands shot to his head while his legs uselessly kicked and flailed behind him. Hector shoved the knife blade less than an inch from Dave's face and screamed at the top of his lungs. Dave went silent and stared at it in shock.

"You see this? You want me to cut your balls off? Keep giving me a hard time and watch what happens," Hector threatened.

Angel looked annoyed. He shoved Zack forward out of the cell and towards the open barn door. For a split-second Zack considered running as fast as his legs would carry him. He knew it was insane, that he'd never make it, but the impulse was so overwhelming it made his skin crawl.

I could never leave my best friend behind, he thought, his heart racing nearly as fast as his thoughts. *I could never live with the guilt if I survived.*

Zack turned back to see that Hector had finally gotten Dave on his feet and was walking him out of the cell. There was a sinking feeling in the pit of his stomach as they passed him, like someone had poured cold cement into his guts.

"Let's go," Angel said, shoving him along. The sun was

already beating down mercilessly on them. The brightness blinded Zack, forcing him to look down to keep from tripping as Angel slowly marched him along. His mind felt oddly clear and empty. He'd run out of ideas on how they were going to escape. All that was left was the sensation of pure fear. He could taste it in his mouth, intense and acidic, like sucking on a fresh battery.

Please God, he thought. *Please help us! Don't let me die here!*

He looked up in surprise to see a dozen young naked women painted up like skeletons, gathered around the Santa Muerte statue. The youngest of them looked no more than twelve years old. Maria stood in front of them holding a ceremonial dagger she'd brought out for the occasion. She nodded at Angel, her silent gesture urging him to bring the hostages to her faster, before turning back to greet her guest of honor. He was not like the other visitors that they had received during their ritual sacrifices. He was a thin, bald man with a well-manicured goatee wearing a suit and collared shirt with the top button undone. He wore expensive designer sunglasses and matching dress shoes with a high mirror shine that reflected the scorching Mexican sun.

"Ramon, I offer you this ceremonial scythe, symbolizing death's unforgiving power over all of mankind," Maria said, handing him her blade. The man set it respectfully at the statues feet.

"I prefer to use my own tools if you don't mind," Ramon said, setting his dark suitcase near the blood stained alter and unlocking it. By the time he had opened the lid the look on Maria's face had gone from accommodating to euphoric. Zack sensed whatever was in the case, whatever had made her that happy to see, couldn't be good for him and Dave. As Angel brought him around to the front of the statue he got a good look inside the briefcase and his suspicions were confirmed. An array of sharp metal tools that included a scalpel, knives, and several metallic motorized devices made it clear that they were not in for a quick and painless death. He fought the urge to piss himself.

"In honor of such a prestigious guest, and devoted follower

of Santa Muerte, I have brought you not one but two American males for your offering to Holy Death," Maria said in a festive tone. "The prayers have already been sung and the offerings have been presented by these anointed virgins. You may begin as soon as you are ready."

Dave began to struggle as the man with the cruel grin approached him, but Hector held him in place with the buck knife to his throat. The hit man took Dave by the face and stared into his eyes looking for something, twisting his jaw back and forth. Dave began to pant but never blinked or took his eyes off the man. When he was done inspecting Dave, the well-dressed killer turned to Zack who immediately stared at the ground.

"Him," the man said, excitement growing in his beady eyes. "I'll start with this one."

Angel walked Zack forward and forced him to his knees in front of the man, leaving him eye level to the man's designer belt logo.

I'm going to die, Zack thought in panic. *He's going to kill me while they all watch!*

"Please," he cried. "Please don't hurt me. Please just let me go."

Zack began to openly weep and beg for his life, which only seemed to excite his executioner more. Reaching into his case full of torture devices Ramon took a curved blade from his briefcase and held it up so Zack could see it.

"Let's start with your eyes," he said. An eerie chill came over Zack as the man began to slowly move the blade towards his face. He squirmed but Angel held him in place. Just as the tip of the knife was about to puncture his iris the sound of a car engine distracted Ramon, causing him to pull back and turn away. Zack gasped, realizing he hadn't been breathing anymore. He looked up to see a police car with the lights on pull up and park a few feet away from them. The cop he'd seen earlier at the resort when they were checking in, Officer Reyes, got out of the driver's side with his gun drawn. All the cult members froze in surprise, but the cartel killer simply smiled. Jamie scurried from the passenger side, her arm extended, her finger pointing at Hector and Angel.

"That's them officer," she said. "Those are the men who took my friends."

"Are you sure?" Officer Reyes asked. "You said you only got a glimpse of them as they carried your friends out."

"I'm positive," she confirmed. He turned back and addressed the crowd.

"What's going on here?" Officer Reyes demanded.

"It's nothing Officer," Maria said with a smile. "Just performing a religious ritual. It's an old local custom."

"Don't listen to her," Jamie yelled. "They kidnapped my friends. Look! They're torturing them! Can't you see? You've got to arrest them!"

Officer Reyes brought his gun up in one clean motion, put the barrel to Jamie's head, and pulled the trigger. Time seemed to slow to a crawl as a bloody rain of brains and skin sprayed out the opposite side of her skull as she toppled over instantly dead. Any hope Zack had been holding onto evaporated as time seemed to stand still. Reyes hesitated a moment before stepping over her body and approaching them.

"Jesus fucking Christ son," he said, looking at Angel. "I'm getting sick and tired of always having to clean up your messes."

"It's not my fault dad," Angel said, shrugging his shoulders. "She wasn't supposed to still be alive. I'll see to it that those responsible pay for this outrage."

Zack watched in horror as Officer Reyes leaned over and planted a big kiss on Maria's lips. The old witch swooned with delight, but the cop pulled back with a concerned look on his face.

"I've been taking a lot of heat about these kids disappearing," Reyes informed her. "I hope this is almost done."

"These are the final sacrifices *Papi*," Maria cooed. "Soon this place will be nothing more than a burning pit of charred and unrecognizable bodies and we'll have moved up the coast without a trace."

"Good," Reyes said. "I don't need any more grief from the Commandante. He's been riding me all morning. If he wasn't so close to the Governor he'd be lined up right next to these pathetic losers after the way he spoke to me."

"All things in due time," Maria said with an evil grin. "Now, let's get back to the business at hand. Carry on, Ramon."

"You are full of surprises," Ramon laughed. The cartel hitman turned to Maria, spinning the shining knife blade around anxiously in his hand like an impatient child. "I like that, but it's time to get back to business if you don't mind."

"Oh yeah," Dave said, finally finding his voice again. Zack spun toward him in surprise. "Let's see how you like this little surprise asshole!"

While the others had been distracted Dave had frantically been working on freeing his hands. There was just enough slack in the leather strap cinched around his wrists to wriggle his wrists together, loosening the bind that kept his hands immobile. Combined with the sweat and oil from his natural secretions Dave had been able to work the straps loose enough to slip out of them altogether. In one quick motion he reached up and grabbed the blade Hector held to his throat, twisting it out of his hands. Hector was so surprised he didn't have time to react before Dave slammed the blade as far into his left eye as it would go. Hector let out a high-pitched howl like a wounded animal, bringing both hands up to his punctured face and backing away squealing.

"Eat shit motherfucker," Dave screamed.

It happened so fast that Zack almost couldn't believe it. Pandemonium spread as a series of lightning quick reactions happened all at once around him. Knowing that their lives depended on his quick thinking and that this was the only chance they'd get to live, Dave didn't waste a single second. He lunged forward and jammed the knife to Angel's throat with one hand, holding him against it with a firmly gripped hand full of hair and causing his neck to snap back. Officer Reyes turned his gun on them, but Dave had moved back behind Angel's bulky frame for cover and he had no clear shot. Reyes cursed with impotent rage, a long string of Spanish words pouring out of him like a hex.

"Untie my friend and let him up," Dave demanded. "Do it or I'll cut his fucking head off. Now!"

Officer Reyes lifted Zack to his feet and gruffly unwound

the leather strap binding his hands together. Zack winced as the blood rushed back into his hands again, wriggling his fingers.

"Now hand him the gun," Dave ordered, forcing the blade against Angel's skin and drawing a trickle of blood to show he was serious.

Officer Reyes handed the weapon over to Zack. The barrel was still warm from shooting Jamie. He looked down at her lifeless corpse. He felt an overwhelming urge to use the gun on the dirty cop for what he'd done, but held back, knowing this would be their only chance to escape.

"I hope you got a good plan to get us out of here Dave," Zack said.

"I'm working on it," Dave said. "Just stay with me."

"What are you doing?" Ramon asked, the note of sheer incredulity in his voice clear as a ringing church bell on a quiet Sunday morning. "You're acting like cowards! Kill them all!"

He turned and threw his curved blade at Angel's head, but he missed. The weapon found another target, sinking up to the hilt in the throat of a nearby cult member. She fell over without a sound and died. Several other female devotees screamed at the top of their lungs. Soon all of them were running back towards the barn, stampeding and trampling one another like panicked animals in a forest fire.

"Nobody threatens my son!" screamed Officer Reyes as he grabbed Ramon by the throat and lifted him off the ground. Ramon looked up at the tall man with a mixture of fear and surprise. Before he could speak Reyes twisted his head with both hands, snapping his neck with a sickening crunch. The feared cartel hitman who had tortured and killed hundreds of innocent and not so innocent people to death for fun and profit was dead before he hit the dirt.

Maria let out a wild cry and rushed at Dave like a feral animal, clawing and scratching him. Dave kicked Angel's legs from underneath him, trying to use him as a shield against the old witch but instead they all toppled to the ground in a pile. Angel wrestled the knife free from Dave and stabbed him in the side, sinking the shining metal all the way in. Dave let out an animal roar as the blade sunk in. Holding the gun with both hands Zack leveled it at Angel and pulled the trigger. The resulting kick caused a jolt of raw pain to shoot up his arms. The gun nearly flew out of his hands, but Zack fought through the pain and held on. The hot slug caught Angel in his right shoulder, causing him to let go of the handle of the buck knife, still neatly lodged firmly into Dave's lower abdomen. Angel scrambled back holding the tender flesh where the bullet had ripped through muscle and lodged in the bone. Officer Reyes advanced on him with a murderous rage in his eyes, but Zack stopped him dead in his tracks by pointing the smoking gun directly in Maria's face.

"One more step and I blow her fucking brains out," Zack assured him, the crazed look in his eyes making it crystal clear he meant exactly what he'd said.

"If you harm one hair on her head," Reyes began but Zack cut him off.

"You'll do what?" His eyes were wild with anger as he spoke. "Torture us to death? Maybe sell us to the highest bidding cartel to be cut into little pieces for your sick devil worship cult? There is nothing left for you to threaten me with so shut the fuck up asshole."

"Hey buddy," Dave said in a strained voice. "I hate to cut you short but I'm losing a lot of blood over here. We need to take this show on the road and fast."

"Stand up," Zack ordered. Maria complied without comment, giving him a dirty look. Zack kept the gun trained on her as he helped his friend to his feet. "Can you make it to the car?"

"I might need a little help," Dave said, looping his arm over his old friend's shoulder.

"You too sweetheart," Zack said, motioning to Maria with the gun. "Let's go."

"You're making a very big mistake," Maria hissed. "The Holy Mother protects and watches over me. She will make you pay for what you've done here."

"Maybe she will and maybe she won't," Zack said, pushing her towards the police cruiser with the barrel of the gun. "Either way you're coming with us. And if any of you try to stop us or slow us down she dies. Got it?"

Officer Reyes just glared in reply. Zack marched her to the cruiser, helping Dave as they went. To his relief the keys were still in the ignition. He'd put on a good show, buoyed up by fear and adrenaline, but he doubted he'd be able to get the keys from Reyes without a fight, one he probably wouldn't survive. He opened the back of the cruiser and motioned for Maria to get inside. She complied with a sneer, a deadly rage covering her features like a widow's veil. Dave slid in next to her, wincing from the pain of the blade still stuck in his side. Zack handed him the gun.

"Keep it on her at all times and don't take your eyes off of her," Zack warned as he climbed into the driver's side. "Any sudden movements on your part and she dies. Understood?"

Reyes nodded, his dark eyes moving back and forth rapidly like a snake.

Zack turned over the ignition and the car roared to life. The sound of the engines smooth purring caused a flood of hope to shoot through him. *We can make it,* he thought in relief. *A few minutes ago, it looked like we were both going to die horrible deaths but now there is a chance we might just survive this nightmare.*

He put the car in gear and backed up slowly, pulling away from the site of the ritual killings. Saint Death leered at him with her bony face as he turned the car, yanking the lever down and putting it into drive. He sped off like a shot being fired out of a cannon, kicking up plumes of dirt and sand as they tore down the unpaved roads before shooting out onto the highway like a bat out of hell.

It was only a matter of minutes before he saw Reyes behind him, racing after them in Angel's black Nissan with the cracked windshield. Zack jammed the gas pedal down as hard as he could, opening a gap between them as they pulled away. He knew it wouldn't last long, that they needed a real plan, but his mind was racing so fast he couldn't think straight.

"What are we going to do?" Dave asked.

"We're going to get you to the hospital," Zack said. "Just hang on."

"We can't go to the hospital," Dave roared. "In a stolen police cruiser? Come on man. Think!"

"We don't have any other options so unless you want to bleed out and die that's my plan," Zack yelled. "We'll just have to pray the rest of the cops aren't in on it. Just sit tight and I'll get you there in one-piece buddy."

They raced down highway 19 back towards Cabo San Lucas, not slowing for cross traffic or stalled vehicles. By the time they had passed the Super Pollo and turned left onto Padre Nicolas Tamaral the Nissan was right on their tail. Angel was in the passenger seat, his right hand cupping his bullet-damaged left shoulder, his eyes locked intently on the cruiser. Reyes sped up and rammed the back of his stolen cruiser with the Nissan, sending a loud vibrating hum through the car's interior.

Dave turned to look back as Reyes punched it again, slamming into them once more. Maria, who had ridden in calculating silence, saw her moment to strike. She grabbed the handle of the buck knife sunk into the soft flesh of Dave's side and twisted it free, causing Dave to let out a blood curdling scream of pain and discharge the gun. Maria blocked his arm as it came up with the gun, forcing it towards Zack's head. The bullet shot through the front windshield narrowly missing Zack's left temple and creating a dazzling spider web of cracked glass as it exited.

"What the fuck?" Zack shouted, his ear ringing so loudly he thought for sure the drum was busted. He turned to see Maria plunging the blade into Dave's stomach several furious times. His friends face turned pale as milk, his expression turning slack. Dave's hand went limp and the gun dropped to the floorboards with a rattle. Holding the wheel with his left-hand Zack swung at Maria in the backseat with his right hand, striking the high priestess in the face. She lashed out at him, thrusting the blade wildly at his neck and slicing into his right ear before burying the blade into Zack's balled up fist. Zack let out a wounded cry, his left hand instinctively jerking the wheel and running them off the road at full speed into the back of a parked car. An explosion of sound erupted as Zack lurched forward against the safety restraint, feeling the belt painfully cut into his chest and stomach. His head whipped around and something heavy and unyielding smacked him in the face, causing him to bite down on his tongue so hard he tasted blood. There was a spray of glass as the windshield exploded and Maria and Dave were ejected. A loud popping sound went off and Zack was thrown back against the seat as the airbag deployed in his face, coating him with white powder and nearly breaking his nose. Somewhere in the distance he heard tires screeching then a loud crash of metal on metal, followed by the near musical tinkle of broken glass raining down on hot asphalt.

Zack sat in shock behind the wheel of the demolished police cruiser, blood drooling from his swollen nose. A warm trickle ran down his neck. He sat up feeling like he'd just survived a kegger at the Frat house, his head ringing, and tried to remember who he was and how he'd gotten there. He reached back and rubbed the blood from his neck, working his way up. A sharp pain rang out as he touched his wounded ear, followed by one in his cut hand. He undid the safety belt and pushed himself out of the cop car.

A small group of people had gathered on the side of the road to point and stare. Zack made his way around the car, limping like a zombie extra on the set of The Walking Dead. Maria and Dave laid about six feet apart, both twisted and motionless, like a child's dolls left out after a particularly rough play session. Zack stumbled quickly towards his friend, doing his best to ignore the blinding pain in his side from where the seat belt had saved his life. His legs felt stiff and his lungs burned. Passing Maria, he saw that her journey through the windshield had nearly decapitated her. A dark pool of crimson oozed around her blood matted hair and face. Her eyes and mouth were open in a state of perpetual surprise. A dark thought occurred to Zack.

Looks like your Saint Death couldn't save you after all, Zack mused, unable to tear his eyes away from the grisly scene of her death. *Hope you enjoy your trip to hell.*

Dave's body looked serene by comparison. His eyes were half closed and there was the slightest hint of a bemused smirk on his lifeless, waxy face.

He was probably already gone by the time he was thrown from the car, Zack realized. *He looks more at peace than I've ever seen him.*

"Well Dave," Zack said, tears welling up in his eyes, "looks like you saved my life buddy. I feel bad that I never got the chance to thank you. I hope you're someplace happy, with your father."

A primal scream brought him out of his dazed reverie. Zack looked up to see Officer Reyes stumbling away from the Nissan, which was now wrapped around a telephone pole on the opposite side of the street.

He lost control right after we did, Zack realized. *Looks like he tried to over correct the wheel and slid into the pole—Angel first.*

He strained but didn't see any movement coming from the passenger side of the car. It certainly didn't look like anyone could possibly have lived through it.

Good, Zack thought defiantly. *Death is what they worshipped, and death is what they deserve.*

Reyes put his head down and charged at him. Zack tried to turn and run but only got a few steps before the enraged officer overtook him with a fierce tackle. The force of the impact took him clean off his feet and the two toppled to the asphalt, rolling over several times before coming to a halt with Reyes on top of the stunned young man. Zack covered his bruised face with his sore hands as a rain of angry blows poured down on him from above. He gasped as Reyes turned his attention to his bruised ribs and tender gut, doubling over onto his side.

"You took everything from me," Reyes raved, sounding like a demon dredged up from the bowels of hell. "Now I'm going to return the favor. After I kill you I'm going to track down the people you love, your parents, your brothers and sisters, and I'm going to make them pay for your crimes against me and my family. Their deaths will be slow and painful, I can promise you that. I will see to it that the women in your family are brutally raped and tortured until they beg for mercy, but I will show them none."

Reyes leaned over and picked his gun up off the asphalt, chambering a fresh round. He cast a long, dark shadow over Zack as he pointed the weapon at his head.

"I will not rest until you and your family are wiped off

the face of the Earth and forgotten," Reyes continued to rant as he stood over Zack, his eyes filled with a delirious fire of righteousness. "There is nowhere the cartel cannot go, no one they cannot get to, even in America. They are in the streets and the prisons. They buy or kill judges, police, even politicians. If your loved ones try to run I will chase them down like animals. You have my word that I will not sleep until they have paid for your sins boy. Think about that as the light fades and *Santa Muerte* eats your eternal soul *cabrón!*"

Zack raised his hands again to his face as Reyes leaned closed with the gun, ready to end his life. A loud crack rang out and Zack let out an involuntary scream as a fine spray of blood covered him. Reyes teetered back and forth in his cowboy boots for a moment before tumbling down on top of Zack. Zack scrambled like a panicked animal to get the dead cop off him, pitching him to the side in his struggle and scurrying to his feet. He stared in confusion at the gaping hole of ragged meat in the middle of Reyes forehead leaking a steady stream of blood, unable to process what had just happened.

"Over here," a voice called out, breaking the spell. Zack looked up to see the limo driver, Oscar, still holding a gleaming fifty caliber revolver with a long shiny barrel and a black rubber grip. In the distance he could hear police sirens. "The cops will be here any minute! Let's go!"

Zack hurried to the limo's passenger side door and climbed in. Oscar got back behind the wheel, tossing the smoking hand cannon between them on the seat. He threw the limo into gear and made a sharp one-hundred-and-eighty-degree turn, driving up over the curb and onto the sidewalk before slamming back down on the road and peeling out.

Zack was still in a daze. "What's happening right now?"

"What's happening is I just saved your life Holmes," Oscar said, taking off his white dress shirt to reveal a wife beater beneath and skin covered with old jail house tattoos.

"But how did you know I was in trouble?" Zack asked.

"I didn't," Oscar said, looking in the rearview nervously. So far, they were still on their own, but Zack knew from the number of bystanders and witnesses that it would only be a matter of time before an APB was put out on the limo. "I told you before, I drive this road a lot for work. I was bringing back a group of kids from Florida but that mess you left in the road back there forced me to stop. When I saw Reyes tackle you I grabbed Eastwood here."

He gently patted his enormous gun with his right hand, the way a proud owner might pet his beloved pure breed after winning Best in Show.

"At that point my fare jumped out and ran," Oscar laughed.

"You named your gun Eastwood?" Zack asked in shock.

"You know," Oscar said, his eyes still locked on the rearview mirror, "like Dirty Harry?"

"I thought you were trying to stay out of prison," Zack said. "Why did you save me?"

"Shit. You could just say thank you," Oscar chided.

"I'm serious," Zack said.

"It's better to do what's right than what's easy," Oscar said. "My grandfather taught me that. He was the most important person in my life. Besides, that cocksucker got what he deserved. Between him and his flunkies demanding payouts several times a week it was becoming almost impossible to make a decent profit anymore. Trust me, a lot of people are going to be happy that he's dead."

"So, what now?" Zack asked nervously.

"I hope you brought your passport," Oscar replied. "Otherwise you're fucked!"

Zack felt in his front pocket. The passport was still there. He took it out and stared at it.

"You said not to trust the hotel staff, so I brought it with me."

"Good," said Oscar, sounding relieved. "We're headed straight to the airport. We'll ditch the car in overnight parking and slip into the terminal. At that point we go our separate ways. I'm going to grab the first flight out of town and I suggest you do the same. Hopefully by the time they realize what's happened you'll be long gone. By the way, what happened to your friend Dave?"

"He didn't make it," Zack said, his eyes filling up again with fresh tears.

Oscar leaned over and opened the glove compartment. Several pill bottles rattled out onto the floorboards as he dug through to find the one he wanted. He popped the lid and brought the bottle to his lips, gulping down a couple pills before handing them to Zack.

"What are they?" Zack asked tentatively, staring at the little yellow pills inside the orange plastic tube.

"Norco," Oscar barked back. "Painkillers. They'll help you get where you're going. Take one now and put the rest in your pocket."

Zack did as Oscar suggested, dry swallowing down the first chalky pill before slipping three more into his jean pocket.

"Thanks man," Zack said. "For everything."

"I'm sorry about your friend," Oscar said. "He was a man after my own heart."

"I can't talk about that right now," Zack said, his eyes filling with stinging tears. "I just can't, or I'll lose it."

"I knew that cop," Oscar said abruptly changing the subject. "He's one of the most corrupt on the force. Who was the woman?"

"His wife I think," said Zack.

"Why was he trying to kill you?" Oscar asked.

"His son drugged and kidnapped us then brought us to some old ranch and sold us to some cartel psychos who were going to torture us to death in some freakish religious ceremony."

"*Santa Muerte*," Oscar whispered, making the sign of the cross over himself. "Saint Death."

Zack's eyes went wide with surprise. "You know about that shit?"

"I've heard rumors," Oscar said, looking concerned for the first time since killing the cop. "They are bad news man. It's said they kill babies and virgins, shit like that, in exchange for power, protection, and in some cases eternal life."

"These guys preferred killing Americans," Zack said. "They got off on it."

"Either way you are lucky to be alive," Oscar said. "Just sit tight. We'll be there soon. Then we roll the dice and pray for luck."

Zack stared out of the window in a daze, fighting back tears. If there was one thing he could use at that moment it was a little bit of luck.

Chapter Fifteen

Zack leaned over the bathroom sink and spit a fresh wad of blood up. He turned on the water, pulling a sip into his mouth, and washing down his second painkiller. Standing back up he gingerly washed the blood off his hands, watching as it turned pink against the slick white basin and whirled down the dark drain. The painkiller had come on strong, blossoming like a warm flower in the middle of his chest that radiated relief. The hot water felt good too. Cautiously he filled his hands with it and began to wash his face and damaged ear. Unrolling a strip of gauze, he began to bandage his ear first and then his hand.

He'd taken the first aid kit from the back of the limo before they'd abandoned it in long term parking as planned. Zack tried to wrap his head around the idea that Oscar was willing to leave behind the life he'd built for himself just to save a stranger's life. He honestly couldn't fathom why he'd done it, and he certainly didn't have the words to adequately thank him, so he stood there awkwardly as Oscar took a couple suitcases from the back of the limo and set them on the parking lot floor.

"I didn't have time to pack a getaway bag," Oscar explained. "Guess I thought I didn't need it anymore since I was out of the life. Lucky for us the guys who bailed on my fare left their stuff behind. Let's see what they left us."

He unzipped the bags and flipped them open. Inside the first were several business suits, dress shirts, and ties. The second contained sportswear. Oscar wasted no time pulling on a Miami Dolphins jersey that read WAKE over the number 91. He found a matching hat inside and pulled it down over his hair all the way to his eyebrows. "How do I look?"

"Like any other red blooded American football fanatic," Zack said. "You should blend right in."

"Perfect," Oscar replied, nodding his head in agreement.

Zack pulled on a long sleeve shirt as delicately as he could then covered it with an expensive suit jacket. Both items were a little oversized, but they'd do so long as he didn't get questioned. He turned back to Oscar who looked oddly excited for a man fleeing a life he'd worked so hard to build.

"I'm taking the suitcase with me," Zack announced. "It might look suspicious if we show up with no luggage."

"Good idea Holmes," Oscar replied, grabbing the sports memorabilia filled duffle bag and looping it over his shoulder. "Well, I guess this is the end of the line for us. Good luck and don't get caught. See you in the next life."

Oscar hurried off through traffic towards the main terminal. After a few minutes had passed, Zack made his way in the same direction, trying his best to blend into the crowd despite looking like he'd just lost a prize fight against Mike Tyson, right down to his torn ear. He hurried into the first bathroom he saw and began the process of cleaning up. He'd been at it for over fifteen minutes. Strangers came and went but none seemed interested in him.

Guess I'm not the first tourist to run into trouble south of the border, Zack thought as he applied the last bandage.

He shut the water off and used wads of fresh paper towels to clean up the bloody residue in the sink. When he was done the results weren't half bad. His nose was still slightly swollen and had a bruise on it, but it wasn't broken as he'd originally suspected. There was the beginning of a fresh shiner starting to form under his right eye but the worst of it wouldn't be fully visible for a couple more days. Other than the covered wounds on his hand and ear he looked like he'd been through no worse than a spirited bar fight.

"All you have to do is get on a plane," Zack told his reflection in the mirror. "There will be time to sort out everything when you're back home safe and sound but if the cops catch you before then you're spending the rest of your life rotting away in a Mexican prison so be fucking cool."

He nodded to himself, took a deep breath, and headed back out into the main terminal. With the suit jacket on and dress shirt over jeans and sneakers he looked like a young professional who'd maybe come down on business and managed to work in just enough recreational time to himself get in an adventure. Scanning across the crowded room he saw several police officers and a few Federales, but none of them seemed worked up. They were busy going about their jobs or simply standing guard, their eyes unblinking, their hands resting idly on their menacing black automatic rifles.

Keep it together, he told himself. *You're almost out of this nightmare.*

He stopped in front of the arrivals and departures board. There were two flights headed back to Los Angeles on American and one on Alaska Airlines. Since they'd come down just the day before on American he thought it might be safer to try returning with a different carrier. He passed a gift store on his way to the ticket counter and ducked inside. He picked up a pair of aviator shades, a few popular magazines, a plush neck pillow, and a computer bag. While the clerk was ringing him up Zack threw in a couple of almond Snickers and a pack of chewing gum.

"Will there be anything else sir?" the clerk asked in a polished voice.

Zack shook his head no. He paid in cash, stuffing the magazines and the pillow into the computer bag. The clerk gave him his change and he slipped the shades on and left eating the candy. He didn't realize how hungry he was, but the candy tasted amazing and the sugar gave him a boost that hit his system right away. By the time he'd made his way over to the Alaska Airlines counter he'd scarfed down both bars. A very young looking Mexican woman with big bright eyes and a wide friendly smile was more than happy to issue him a ticket.

"How many bags are you checking today sir?" she asked.

"Just the one," he said, putting the bag he'd taken from the back of the limo up on the scale. He patted the new computer bag he'd just bought and smiled at her. "I'm taking this one with me as my carry on."

"Perfect," the perky brunette said, putting her hand out for his passport. He did his best to keep his hand from shaking as he passed it to her. Zack felt her eyes briefly roam from his face to his hands as she entered his passport information into her computer. Her well-manicured nails raced over the keys, clicking away like a snake's rattle. She paused suddenly, and he held his breath. She looked up and he felt like his heart was going to jump out of his chest.

She's on to me, he thought suddenly, the urge to drop everything and run rising back up in him like a deadly viper. He casually glanced around trying to decide on the best escape route should it come to that but saw little hope. There were too many witnesses, too many people swarming through the airport for him to make a clean get away. They would be on him in seconds if he bolted. He was sure of it. If they took him in he'd never see any of the people he loved ever again, including his parents.

"Sir?" Zack turned back to the woman behind the counter. She smiled politely, and he felt the stitch in his chest relax just slightly. "I said how would you like to pay?"

"Try this one," Zack said, his voice trembling as he tried to remain calm. He slid a credit card across the counter to her. "I can use the points."

She took the card without hesitation and ran it through her machine with a swipe of her delicate wrist. He held his breath as she waited for approval. He expected at any moment a swarm of armed Federales to descend on him, automatic weapons drawn, ready to take down a wanted cop killer. Instead the machine erupted in a series of beeps as it spit out a new boarding pass. The young woman tore part of the pass off and wrapped it around his suitcase handle before placing it on a conveyor behind her. She slipped the paper ticket into a folded booklet and handed it to him.

"Your flight is already boarding at gate seven," she said with a beaming smile. "Have a nice trip home!"

"Thank you," he replied, already slinking away with his new computer bag tucked under his arm. He held his passport and the boarding pass in his sweaty palm and tried to look casual as he made his way towards gate seven and got in line. Glancing at the mirror overhead he saw a series of police officers walking side by side up the terminal. He felt the pit of his stomach drop out as he saw them fan out and begin searching the gates. The urge to turn and run came crashing over him like a rogue wave, but his feet wouldn't cooperate. They felt nailed to the floor. Any minute now they would be on him.

"Ticket please," a voice close to him said, shaking him back to reality. Zack looked up to see the male flight attendant with his hand out waiting for his pass.

"Here," was all he could manage to say as he willed his hand to rise and hand the passport and boarding pass to the overly chipper attendant.

"*Gracias amigo,*" the man smiled, tearing the back end off the pass and running it through a machine. He handed it to back to Zack. "You're all set. Welcome aboard sir."

Zack stumbled forward clumsily feeling like a man who'd been pardoned at the last minute for a second time. There was a fat woman in an obscenely short yellow dress arguing with a female flight attendant near the entrance to the plane, causing the line of people boarding to slow down. Zack turned back cautiously to sneak a peek at the terminal behind him. There was a loud commotion, followed by yelling and a woman's high pitch screams. Zack strained to see what the source of the commotion was. Several of the officers had tackled a man to the ground and were wrestling with him to get their suspect under control. Zack felt his stomach muscles clench up as he waited in anticipation. After what felt like a small eternity they lifted the man up to his feet. Zack saw at once that it was Oscar. They were patting him down when Zack heard a woman's voice behind him.

"Excuse me," the female attendant sweetly sang. "We need for you to take your seat please."

Zack turned to see that the line of people in front of him had cleared and now he was holding up several anxious passengers trying to board. They glared at him in annoyance. He quickly turned back to the flight attendant.

"Sorry," he said in a deep voice, turning and marching onto the plane.

Chapter Sixteen

He was back home in his own childhood bed. The doorbell was ringing loudly again and again. He sat up and stretched, looking around. His parents had left everything the exact same way he'd left it when he went off to college, right down to the Ferrari and Lamborghini posters on the wall with bikini models draped over the exotic cars. Warm sunlight beamed in through his bedroom window.

Must be well into the afternoon, Zack thought as he stretched and basked in the warmth. *Maybe that's why no one is home to answer the door.*

He got up and pulled on a pair of freshly washed jeans. One thing he loved about coming home from school was having clean clothes all the time. Living on campus he was lucky if he managed to do laundry once a week. His mom, on the other hand, did several loads every single day. He lifted his shirt and inhaled. The fabric was soft and clean and smelled like perfume.

Ocean breeze, he thought as he pulled it on over his head. *That's what the company who makes the fabric softener calls it, but it smells more like flowery lotion than anything.*

The doorbell was still ringing as he stumbled out of his room and down the hallway past his little sister Gwen's room. At sixteen she was one of the most popular kid in his high school which meant she wasn't around much, but when she was the door would be closed with either Demi Lovato or Taylor Swift cranked up behind it. *A secret world none of us can ever really penetrate or understand,* he thought. His sister's door was now wide open, and he could see her dirty clothes strewn on the floor as he passed.

The doorbell didn't slack. It kept ringing over and over, the sound somehow growing louder as it did.

"I'm coming," he groused, gingerly padding down the hallway towards the door. He'd been lost in the most realistic dream, something about a beach vacation gone wrong with his best friend, but it was slipping away from him in pieces. The more he struggled to remember details the faster it faded.

It had something to do with Mexico, he vaguely recalled. *And Dave was in it. And there was a beautiful girl, but I can't remember her name, just her face.*

The doorbell grew louder still, accompanied now by a series of fierce knocks that made Zack's stomach churn in dread.

"I said I'm coming," Zack shouted, reaching for the shiny knob.

He threw the door open, but no words came out. Standing before him on his parent's porch covered in blood and broken glass from head to toe was none other than Angel. His eyes burned with a murderous rage as he sprang at Zack with both hands out, knocking him on his back. Zack punched and kicked at him, but it was no use. It was like Angel was made from some foreign, unyielding metal that seemed to suck all the energy from inside of him. Angel wrapped his stubby fingers around Zack's throat and began to choke the life out of him.

"You cannot escape us," Angel laughed, his voice now a dark, demonic rattle. "There is nowhere you can run, no place on Earth or hell you can hide that we won't find you. You're going to pay for what you did! YOU'RE WHOLE FAMILY IS GOING TO PAY!"

Zack fought with all his might, but it was no use. He was slipping away, his eyes bulging out of his head as he fought for air. Looking over Angel's shoulder he saw Reyes and Maria appear in ghostly form, their bodies made from a swirling mass of black clouds. They laughed at Zack's pain and goaded their evil son on.

"Drink in his suffering," Maria cackled, her face contorting into dark smoke.

"Finish him off son," Officer Reyes urged as Angel clamped his hands down with all his strength, crushing Zack's windpipe.

As he lay there waiting for death to take him Reyes leaned down until their faces were almost touching, ice cold tendrils of hellish black smoke coiling off him like writhing serpents.

"I told you," he boomed, a flickering serpent's tongue flicking in and out of his mouth. "You're going to pay for what you did to my family, starting with your little sister."

A burst of energy from deep inside of him exploded and he began to thrash around once more, kicking and punching and screaming at the top of his lungs.

"NOOOOO!!!"

Zack shot up in his seat and nervously looked around. His hand and his ear throbbed with pain. The roar of the plane's engines was a steady rumble that brought him back to reality. He looked down to see that he'd bled through his hand bandage and a crimson trail was leaking down his hand and dripping on the plastic covered aisle lights. When he gazed back up he saw an old white guy wearing a cowboy hat staring at him with amusement from across the aisle.

"Looks like you were having one hell of a dream," the man guffawed. "You were thrashing around punching the armrest and mumbling to yourself."

"Where are we?" Zack asked in a stupor.

"Good old You Ess of Eh. Just crossed over the border," the man replied matter-of-factly. "We're out over the ocean just past San Diego or thereabouts. Shouldn't be long now until we land back at LAX. I hope it doesn't take too long to get through customs. I've got dinner plans in Calabasas."

"Excuse me," Zack said, unfastening his lap belt and headed back towards the lavatories. He passed the overly-friendly male flight attendant who'd taken his ticket.

"Sir the fasten seat belts sign is still on," the airline employee informed him with an exaggerated sigh. "Can you please return to your seat until the Captain turns it off. Sir!"

Zack didn't respond. He slid into the open bathroom and locked the door behind him. Reaching carefully into his front right pocket he fished the last of the painkillers out and popped them in his mouth, rinsing them down with some water from the sink. Carefully he unwound the soiled bandage on his hand

and stared at the gaping puncture wound.

It looks like a little red mouth, he thought absentmindedly as he watched the fresh blood pool back into the gash admiring the way it glistened.

He'd need stitches, no doubt about it, but as far as he was concerned that was a problem he could live with. He'd survived. So long as the plane didn't crash before they got back to LAX he was going to be okay.

"I'm alive," he said, his voice shaky as he let the words sink in. "Dear God, I made it out alive."

He sat on the toilet and began to sob as he waited for the little yellow pills to kick in and wash his memory away.

Afterword

I had the original idea to write *Saint Death* back in 2004 as a screenplay. I'd just written and sold a horror script called "Shock Therapy" that never ended up seeing the light of day, despite being shot and edited as part of a seed deal for a major Hollywood studio. Although I knew the basic plot line I was missing many of the details that would coalesce over the next decade to make it a reality as the short novel you (presumably) just read. Among them are my travels through Mexico including a road trip from Nogales to Saylita, an unforgettable trip to Cabo San Lucas, and my time in Puerto Vallarta.

While I never had any experience more sinister than petty theft befall me in my travels through Mexico, and the vast majority of people I encountered were friendly and kind, not everyone visiting from the United States has the same to say about their time south of the border. There actually are dozens of websites online that describe the types of police corruption I portray in Saint Death, and unfortunately, they report shake downs and scams like the ones I describe in nearly every single popular beach town in Mexico. A simple internet search of Cabo San Lucas will reveal elements I cribbed to spin this yarn for a more realistic feel. Though far-fetched at points it might have seemed it was, believe it or not, always based on real events.

I was also influenced by the horrifying true story of Adolfo Constanzo, a black magic practitioner in Mexico City who performed grim sacrificial rituals on behalf of cartel bosses and their hit men to supposedly make them invincible against police and impervious to bullets. Along with his appointed High Priestess Sara Maria Aldrete their cult sold voodoo protection packages to superstitious gangsters for around $40,000 a pop.

The evil duo's reign of terror ended when, working on their behalf, a group of their devotees abducted an American college student named Mark Kilroy from outside a bar in Mexico he was partying at while on Spring Break. Kilroy was brought to the cult's ranch and sacrificed. When the Mexican authorities eventually raided the property, they discovered fifteen chopped up human bodies buried on the premises. Constanzo died in a literal hail of bullets, by his own request, and Aldrete surrendered and was given sixty years in prison.

And then there is the Skinny Lady herself, Saint Death. I became aware of Santa Muerte over the last few years from news articles and pop culture references like the infamous one in Breaking Bad. I decided the growing practice of her worship, particularly the darker aspect that has emerged, would make a great post for my bimonthly horror column Dark Dreams on The Escapist. I've included that article here at the end so you the reader can see just how real and terrifying the worship of Saint Death can be when it takes this darker form. As you will see much of what I learned in my studies was incorporated into the story itself, and rightly so. It is chilling in an unimaginable way and proves yet again that reality is far scarier than anything a horror writer could ever dream up.

Devan Sagliani
9/04/15

DARK DREAMS:

The Rise in Popularity of Saint Death

Nacozari, Mexico is a quiet little copper mining town nestled into the northeast part of Sonora, not far from the U.S. Border crossing in Nogales. The last time anyone bothered to do a census, back around the turn of the century, the humble city boasted just over fourteen thousand residents, a fair number who were both poor and living in shacks. 44-year-old Silvia Meraz, along with seven people associated with her, were among these destitute—including her boyfriend Eduardo Sanchez, her father, her son, three daughters and a daughter-in-law. In fact, they were so poor that both the government and the church regularly took pity on them, offering free food, used clothes and even farm animals. The men were known to dig through the trash looking for scraps of food or valuable items they could resell while many of the women were presumed to be prostitutes. Mexican officials became suspicious that Meraz was using her residence for sex tourism after seeing strange men from out of town frequently visiting, but never gathered enough evidence to arrest anyone.

When Martin Rios, a 10-year-old boy, went missing in July 2010, his mother told authorities that friends of theirs had seen him begging in the streets near the border of Douglas, Arizona. After searching for months there was still no sign of him. He was never seen again. In early March of 2011 another 10-year-old boy, Jesus Martinez, went missing, prompting Sonora State's missing persons unit to send a couple agents to Nacozari to find out what was going on. They discovered that the boys knew several of the same people. Martin Rios was the son of the ex-girlfriend of Sanchez. Jesus Martinez was the step-grandson of Meraz. Both boys were frequent visitors at Meraz's residence on the outskirts of town. Desperate for answers the agents began to put pressure on Meraz and her family until one of them slipped up or admitted what they knew. Eventually their persistence paid off.

In 2012 agents unearthed the body of Jesus Martinez, which had been buried in the dirt floor in the bedroom of one of the Meraz daughters. Afterward they arrested all seven family members, who went on to lead the agents to the remains of Rios and the grave of 55-year-old Cleotilde Romero, one of Meraz's closest friends who had vanished without a trace after they'd had an argument back in 2009. Both bodies were buried near the shack where the murderous cult members lived. According to their official report the victims' throats and wrists had been slashed so that the blood could be collected and spread on a sacrificial altar.

The Sonora Attorney General's Office named Silvia Meraz as the cult leader after she and the rest of the family identified themselves as devotees of the patron Saint of Death, Santa Muerte. Meraz confessed to the media that she was indeed a practitioner of blood magic and that she deeply believed their protector would bring them money and power. Instead she brought misery and suffering down upon all their heads.

"What can she do for us?" Meraz cried to reporters in between unleashing a string of profanities. "Nothing."

Nuestra Señora de la Santa Muerte—more commonly known as Santa Muerte or "Saint Death"—is a female folk saint venerated primarily in Mexico and the United States within Latino communities, despite fierce opposition from the Catholic Church. The origins of her cult have roots that delve far back into the deep history of Mexican folk culture and superstitions, blending indigenous Mesoamerican traditions with newer Catholic beliefs introduced by the Spanish. After the Spanish conquest of the Aztec Empire, the conquerors did their best to bring an end to pagan forms of the worship of death but were never completely able to eradicate it. It simply was too ingrained in the culture to be forgotten. Researchers have recently discovered references dating back to 18th-century Mexico, recorded during the Spanish Inquisition, when a group of indigenous people in central Mexico tied up a skeletal figure they addressed as "Santa Muerte" and threatened it with violence unless it performed miracles and granted their deepest wishes. Unlike Dia de los Muertos—the Day of the Dead—a festive holiday that commemorates death as a natural part of the cycle of life, Santa Muerte is a darker practice more recently popularized by drug lords, cartel hitmen, and other outlaws who worship and make offerings to the personification of death for healing, protection, wealth, glory, and in some cases, the hope of eternal life here on Earth.

Santa Muerte is known by many different names including Señora de las Sombras ("Lady of the Shadows"), Señora Blanca ("White Lady"), Señora Negra ("Black Lady"), Niña Santa ("Holy Girl"), Santa Sebastiana (St. Sebastienne) or Doña Bella Sebastiana ("Our Beautiful Lady Sebastienne") and the most popular one—La Flaquita ("The Skinny Little Lady"). A skeletal female figure most often clad in a long robe and wedding dress, she usually carries a scythe in one hand and a globe in the other. Some practitioners adorn her in garish displays of expensive jewelry or lavish robes in alluring arrays of colors depending on the aspect being worshipped. She may appear forebodingly clad from head to toe in black as well.

No matter how she manifests this increasingly popular folk saint specializes in protecting followers from their enemies and striking down those they wish to harm. By turns jealous and vengeful, the personification of death who does not judge but leads the faithful who properly conduct sacrifices and rituals safely to the afterlife, is rapidly growing a following among the infamous drug cartels of Mexico as well as working-class professionals.

Prior to the 20th century most prayers and other rites to the Death Saint were secretly performed in the privacy of the practitioner's home. Since the turn of the 21st century worship has become more acceptable and public, especially in Mexico after a shrine was created for Santa Muerte in Mexico City in

2001. The number of believers in Santa Muerte has mushroomed in the past ten years. Authorities now believe as many as eight million people openly worship the folk icon, making Saint Death the second only to Saint Jude, and putting her into direct competition with the country's beloved Virgin of Guadalupe. The meteoric rise in the size of the death cult is believed to be connected to her supposed ability to quickly grant wishes and perform miracles as well as the surge in drug violence.

Among the poor, where her worship has exploded in recent years, which is not surprising since she offers hope for the chance of a better life to those who sing her praises. Worship has been seen to peak during times of economic crisis with many followers being young, female, and disillusioned with the established Catholic Saints ability to deliver them from the miseries of the abject poverty they exist in. But the cult of Santa Muerte is present throughout all the strata of Mexican society, not just urban working-class families, who constitute most devotees. Military and police agents, elected officials, artists, and other affluent members of Mexican society have been identified as secret practitioners in recent years.

In 2001, a devotee named Enriqueta Romero took her life-sized image of Santa Muerte from her home in Mexico City and built a shrine that was visible from the street, shocking her neighbors and drawing people from all over Mexico to come pray and to leave offerings for the Lady of Death. Every year on November 1, thousands of people descend on her rough neighborhood in Tepito to celebrate the adopted holiday, clutching skeletal dolls that depict their protector, who is dressed as a bride and adorned with gold for the celebration. A carnival-like atmosphere pervades Santa Muerte's most important ceremony of the year, with food, music and dancing well into the night as well as sex and drugs.

Still a surprisingly number of worshipers of "the Bony Lady" consider themselves to be devout Catholics, despite praying to a non-canonized folk saint openly repudiated and demonized by the Church. In a country where the dominant religion is Catholicism the rituals and processions of the worship of Saint Death take on a decidedly familiar tone, either in deference or in mockery. Self-appointed priests replace the traditional hierarchy the same way marijuana smoke replaces ceremonial incense. There are temples and shrines as well as other ritualized elements that effectively merge traditional forms of veneration with their local beliefs and customs.

The Church has been unequivocal in its response, stating that devotion to Santa Muerte "is the celebration of devastation and of hell" and that practice should be stomped out with the help of families and communities. Still worship continues to grow among their followers, owing in part to Saint Death's supposed ability to quickly grant wishes and her lack of judgement, the latter being the more likely draw for gang members and outlaws. In a country plagued by drug violence, worship of the malleable and forgiving Saint has at times taken on a more deadly and sinister form—reflecting the violent struggle many of them face daily for survival. While most followers are engaged in benign practices involving nothing more than making offerings and prayers to 'the Skinny One' this nefarious element has taken up their own form of Santa Muerte worship, reimagining the often-maligned saint as a darker icon with an unquenchable thirst for blood.

In an interview with the BBC Father Ernesto Caro blames Santa Muerte for the rise in exorcisms, claiming that the practice is "the first step into Satanism" and that drug traffickers and killers routinely offer Flaquita sacrifices. Some cartels insist their members practice their twisted version of Santa Muerte worship, using devotion as a tool to control their foot soldiers and turning gruesome killings into religiously sanctioned offerings to the figure of death herself. One such individual, a cartel hitman charged with disposing of victim's bodies, came to be exorcised at Caro's church in Monterrey. Believing he was possessed by demons he gleefully divulged how he'd cut up bodies and burned others alive, relishing the sounds of their tortured screams as they died. When asked why he took such delight in the suffering of others the man explained he was a devote follower of Santa Muerte. Father Caro insists this is not an isolated incident but rather is becoming the new norm.

"Santa Muerte is being used by all our drug dealers and

those linked to these brutal murders," Caro explained to the BBC. "We've found that most of them, if not all, follow Santa Muerte."

In a country where drug-related violence has swallowed up over 150,000 people in the last decade, including innocent bystanders, the appeal of the dark worship of an amoral deity who offers protection, wealth, status, and power is as intoxicating as the narcotics driving the brutality. Faced with the near certainty of a grisly death at the hands of their enemies, some cartel members have begun offering severed body parts including human heads, rather than the traditional beer or tobacco, hoping to invoke some form of divine intervention by rubbing cocaine and human blood on their Santa Muerte statues. In one instance a vicious cartel killer boasted that Santa Muerte had brought him back from death five times, right before two enforcers hacked him to pieces with machetes.

In Tepito it was discovered that a drug lord was holding annual human sacrifices of virgins and newborns in return for the Saint bestowing magical powers on him. Recently a mass grave was unearthed in the drug crime embattled northern state of Sinaloa. All 50 bodies were marked with symbols and adornments depicting Santa Muerte. Although venerated alongside Jesús Malverde, the "Saint of Drug Traffickers" whose following is strong in his hometown of Sinaloa, the force of Santa Muerte is much more dominant. Altars with images of Santa Muerte have begun to crop up routinely in raided drug houses in both Mexico and the United States, as immigrants bring their practices with them to their new homes.

Churches for Santa Muerte have cropped up in San Francisco, Chicago, New York City, and New Orleans, as well as other heavily populated areas that draw in migrant workers. At present there are 15 religious groups in Los Angeles alone dedicated to her worship and not just by Latinos. Increasingly larger numbers have begun to show up at pseudo-religious ceremonies as the worship of the celebrated folk Saint continues to spread inside the United States. Each day millions of people pray to her, asking for her assistance in both worldly and spiritual matters, including cartel and gang members who in some cases ask for nothing more than a quick, painless death and for their names to live on in glory long after they are gone.

For more information on Santa Muerte check out Devoted to Death by Andrew Chesnut, the leading authority on the growing cult. Until next time... Stay Scared!

Devan Sagliani

@devansagliani—Twitter, Facebook & Instagram

http://devansagliani.com
http://smarturl.it/devansagliani
Originally published on The Escapist at http://www.escapistmagazine.com/articles/view/comicsandcosplay/columns/darkdreams/14021-Santa-Muerte-Gaining-More-Prominence-in-Mexican-Culture

Acknowledgements

First and foremost, I would like to thank my wife, Angie. Your unceasing support for my passion gives me the strength I need to fight through the dark moments of doubt as a writer and stay true to my voice. I love you baby.

Thanks also to the Salerno family for their love and support, especially Mama Salerno, who took it upon herself to be both my willing and eager beta reader as well as my first editor. I appreciate your love and support more than you can ever know.

Thanks as well to C.T. Phipps for showing me and my work great kindness in the past. Thanks to Dave Gammon for my first great review and for always supporting me as well.

Thanks to Dean Samed for the beautiful cover.

Thanks as well to Alexander Macris from DEFY Media who persuaded me that doing a bimonthly horror column for a gamer site was a good idea. Thanks to Clive McLean who first introduced me to Cabo San Lucas. You and your stinky cigars are missed by all who knew and loved you, Seen Yor Cleave Eh.

Lastly, thanks to you, my incredible readers, for supporting my work. I love receiving feedback from readers and connecting with them on social media. I also love seeing your positive and encouraging reviews. They help more than you can know. So please, friends, if you enjoyed Saint Death, leave a review on Amazon for me. Thanks again.

About the Author

Devan Sagliani was born and raised in Southern California and graduated from UCLA. He is the author of the bestselling *Zombie Attack* series, the *Undead L.A.* series, *The Rising Dead, A Thirst For Fire, Saint Death, Poseidon Pier,* and more. His screenwriting credits include *Humans Vs. Zombies* and *Shock Therapy*.

His fiction has been nominated for the Pushcart Prize and the Million Writers Award. In 2012 *Zombie Attack* won Best New Horror Novel on Goodreads. *The Rising Dead* and *Zombie Attack* were both named on the Best Zombie Books of 2015 by Ranking Squad.

For more on his work visit his official website at:

http://evansagliani.com.

Visit him on social media at:

http://www.twitter.com/devansagliani
&
http://www.facebook.com/ZombieAttackRiseOfTheHorde.

Curious about other Crossroad Press books?
Stop by our site:
http://store.crossroadpress.com
We offer quality writing
in digital, audio, and print formats.

Enter the code FIRSTBOOK
to get 20% off your first order from our store!
Stop by today!

www.ingramcontent.com/pod-product-compliance
Lightning Source LLC
Chambersburg PA
CBHW061250170626
46809CB00007B/2933